# Alias

# Alias

Mary Elizabeth Ryan

ALADDIN PAPERBACKS

First Aladdin Paperbacks edition November 1998
Text copyright © 1997 by Mary Elizabeth Ryan

Aladdin Paperbacks
An imprint of Simon & Schuster Children's Publishing Division
1230 Avenue of the Americas
New York, NY 10020

Also available in a Simon & Schuster Books for Young Readers hardcover edition.
The text for this book was set in Mrs. Eaves.
Printed and bound in the United States of America
10 9 8 7 6 5 4 3

The Library of Congress has cataloged the hardcover edition as follows:
Ryan, Mary E.
Alias / by Mary Elizabeth Ryan.
p.   cm.
Summary: Fifteen-year-old Toby, who has spent his entire life traveling from place to place with his mother as she constantly changes her identity, discovers that she is a political fugitive from justice.
ISBN 0-689-80789-9 (hc)
[1. Fugitives from justice—Fiction. 2. Mothers and sons—Fiction.]
I. Title.
PZ7.R955Al   1997   [Fic]—dc20   96-34184   CIP   AC
ISBN 0-689-82264-2 (pbk)

for Brent

I am on a train, like the ones in the movies, with paneled compartments and old-fashioned seats. The train takes a curve, and I see out the window that at the edge of the track there's . . . nothing. I grip the edge of the seat, knowing if I move an inch, the whole train, the whole track—*everything*—will fall off the cliff, into black emptiness: the end of the world.

When I woke up, I felt stiff and sore. My hand was clutching the metal hinge of the sofa bed. I'd been having that dream for years. I wondered where it came from, what it meant. It always gave me the sick feeling that *everything was up to me*—if I made a false move, the game was over.

Then the alarm clock jangled, and I remembered—with a twist in my chest—what was supposed to happen today.

Forget the lousy dream. If I pushed it, I'd have time for instant coffee and a doughnut.

Mom had already left for her job as a cashier at a flower shop downtown, near the big hotels. It wasn't much of a job, but it explained the smell that hung over the Dumpster, our one-bedroom apartment: The place was crammed with flowers. Most nights Johnny, Mom's boss, let her take the surplus flowers home. Mom's a genius when it comes to plants. They were all over the living room and the kitchen counter.

I boiled water and stirred in some coffee powder, shoving aside Mom's African violets to make room for a cup. Too bad she couldn't find a dog or a cat that needed a home, instead.

Not that it made any difference—the slumlord who owned this place wouldn't let the inmates keep pets. When I was nine, I got to have a puppy once. That was six years ago, in another city in another state. Brewster was long gone, wriggling out the door one day never to return. There had been a lot of other states since then.

And now we were in sunny L.A., where the apartments had iron bars over the windows, and every now and then a car slowed outside, and you woke thinking it was the Fourth of July. Until you figured out those pops weren't firecrackers.

I swallowed the coffee in one gulp and grabbed my books. Phantom would be waiting. "You'd better be there," he'd said.

The past few months avoiding the Phantom had become a way of life. Today I planned to skip out last period before I had to give a report on ancient Egypt. I hadn't done much research anyway. I figured if they needed to know about dead pharaohs, they could dig up King Tut.

I waited until the bell rang. Then I slipped into the boys' room in case the vice principal was patrolling the halls for truants.

Two older kids were in there, peddling pot to a freshman. I ignored them and pretended to study a stray zit.

My face looked flat and blank in the mirror, like the face of the moon, or some lifeless planet. Dishwater-blond hair hung over the tops of my huge ears, which matched my huge feet. I felt like one of those bargain-basement suits where the jacket's too short and the pants are too long—a misfit.

The only good thing about my face were my eyes. Blue and sharp. Mom's are a deep brown. I had enough biology at my last school to know that blue eyes come from a recessive gene. Meaning that somewhere out there, on my father's side, I've got a bunch of recessive, blue-eyed cousins. With huge ears and feet.

"Toby Chase?" I turned away from the mirror.

The bathroom was empty. Then I looked closer, and saw Phantom's size twelves under one of the stalls.

I couldn't see him, but I knew he could see me, that he was watching me from the other side of the scratched metal door. I stuck a Don't Mess With Me sign on my face, but inside I was scared. He'd been after me all year: Sell this for me, give that kid what's in the bag, drop something here, go there, keep half for yourself.

So far all I'd done was buy time. But now Phantom wanted me to drag someone else into it. That was how it worked. I hated knowing he wanted to make me feel afraid. If it wasn't for Mom, I might have taken off by now. But I couldn't do that to her. I was all she had.

And it was all about to explode.

"Did you talk to Teddy?" The voice was low, a rusty hinge on an invisible door.

Teddy Lee was a nice little kid in my homeroom. Little Teddy didn't stand a chance.

"Haven't seen him," I said. Stupid, but brave.

Something metal struck the stall door. The crash echoed off the tiles. I winced.

I didn't stick around to find out what it was. In a second I was out of the bathroom, down the stairs, and out the door of Fillmore High.

Mary Elizabeth Ryan

Well, almost out the door. Just as I reached the exit, a big hand attached itself to my shoulder.

"Going somewhere, Mr. Chase? School's not out for forty-five minutes."

It was Mr. Boyer—Fillmore's Joe Friday, the Kindergarten Cop himself.

I switched on my default expression: blank smile. "Got a doctor's appointment."

Boyer peered at me. "You don't look sick to me," he said.

"Eye doctor appointment," I improvised, squirming away from the vice principal's viselike fingers. "Can't see the board. Probably need glasses."

He sighed and let go of my shoulder. "You look like a bright kid, Toby," he said. "Got a future, college waiting for you. You don't want to spoil it with 'delinquent' all over your record."

"I think the word is 'truant,'" I corrected him. "I'm not into vandalism, or drug dealing, or any of the popular team sports here at Fillmore." It was true; he couldn't argue the point.

"Your mom's a nice lady," he said finally. "I don't want to put her through another long talk about what to do with you. She always looks so sad."

My eyes grazed the space behind him. A dark

shape moved like a whisper down the hall.

For a moment I considered telling Boyer what was going on. Phantom would figure I had snitched anyway.

Boyer was still studying me. Then something in his eyes swung shut, and the moment passed.

I was doomed.

"So straighten up, buddy. End of chat. Now get back to class. March!"

Boyer was blocking the exit door with his cheap suit, so I did the smart thing. I shrugged, snapped off a salute, and marched.

"Another day, another pharaoh," I called.

Joe Friday didn't get it, and I didn't care.


To be safe I took the long way home. Practically through the next county. But the minute I walked in the door and tossed down my books, I didn't feel safe anymore.

Something was different.

Then I nailed it: The plants were gone.

And not just the plants. All the paperbacks had been scooped off the shelf next to the TV. The TV was unplugged, the cord wrapped around it like an electrical vine.

"Mom?" I called, panic filling my voice as I headed down the hall. *"Mom?"*

"In here, Toby," she called from the bedroom. A pile of clothes covered Mom's bed, hangers poking out every which way.

"What's going on?" I asked, even though I already knew the answer.

She was inside the closet, tossing skirts and blouses through the air. When she came out, I saw there was something different about Mom, too.

That didn't surprise me, either—my mom's always trying out new looks. For over a year she'd worn her hair tied in a long braid down her back. Now it was short and curly. She keeps herself in pretty good shape, but not really muscular. The short hair looked good on her. I wondered how long she'd keep it that way.

"Don't tell me," I said, keeping my voice deadpan. "Let me guess. We're, uh, moving again?"

She shot me an exasperated look and then smiled. I couldn't tell whether it was a real one, or just something to sweeten me up. My mom can be a real con artist when she wants to be.

"For heaven's sake, Toby—don't tell me you wanted to stay here?"

"God, no." I plopped down on the bed, making the clothes bounce. "But school doesn't let out for a few months. Boyer won't like it. . . ."

"We won't *ever* have to worry about Mr. Boyer

again," she said. "I've got it all figured out."

She reached for a plastic garbage bag, the kind you could fit an elephant inside, and began shoving clothes into it: Mom's idea of luggage. She scrubbed a hand through her new short hair. She'd colored it, too—it was light brown now, instead of dark.

"Nice dye job," I remarked. "Washed that gray away?"

"Helen at the salon talked me into it," Mom said.

She tossed me the garbage bag and threw down a last armful of clothes. "And now, smart guy, I'm going to wash this horrible town out of my pores. First a shower, and then we'll hit the road."

"Sounds like a plan," I said. "Hey, is there anything to eat around here?" I called as she headed for the bathroom. "Or have you packed up the refrigerator, too?"

"There's salami, I think, and some bread," she called back as the shower swished on. "Make me a sandwich, too, will you, Toby? I really want to beat that traffic."

I headed for the kitchen, but the last thing on my mind was making a sandwich. I could hear the train from my dream, the shriek of its whistle as it rattled along the edge . . . I thought about the

Phantom, and firecrackers reaching into your sleep.

Outside a car slowed, and I froze.

It moved on. Just a red light, I told myself. But when I reached for the bread, I had another thought: For once, I was definitely ready to move.

Then again, if you had Annie Chase for a mom, you didn't have much choice.

After we ate, Mom left to run some errands. I got out my duffel bag and began to pack.

There wasn't much. Some clothes, a few books, my tape player. When I was done, I sat down with my trusty skateboard on my lap, spinning the wheels with one hand while I waited for Mom.

I wondered where we were going, and how we were going to get there. Not that it mattered; when the urge to move hit, Mom never gave much warning.

I looked around at the Dumpster. I sure wouldn't miss camping out in the living room on a sofa bed.

Or school. I grinned, picturing what Phantom would do when he found out I'd split. Then I stopped grinning. Too bad for Teddy—I wished I could warn him.

Too bad for me, too. Now Boyer could add "dropout" to my resume, along with "poor attitude," "truant," "doesn't respect authority." Maybe if I'd told him about Phantom, he might have understood. But then he would have told Mom.

Things hadn't gone much better at my last school, in Tennessee, and they'd never called Mom once. Then again, Nashville was a much cooler town, with country music all over the place, and the funny way people drawled. I'd almost hated to leave.

Mom had worked as a secretary for a tire company—"Tired Tires," she used to call it. The minute Mom's job drove her nuts, bang—off we'd go.

Other times it was the climate—it rained too much in Seattle, Florida was too hot, Boston was bad for her allergies. Or the economy, or the traffic, or the rent was to blame. I never argued. When you moved around as much as we did, places started to seem alike.

I got up to make another sandwich. The salami was gone, but there was some peanut butter. My school books were still lying on the counter. I glanced at them, then tossed them in the bag headed for the trash.

No point taking those—every school taught things a different way. Just when I was getting the hang of multiplication tables, we'd split, and there went nine times nine, off in the ozone with the other stuff I never learned. But by the time I was ten, I was pretty good at geography.

I wasn't good at making friends. Everywhere we moved, the kids were a closed circle. End of story.

One place, a carnival came to town right after we moved there, and before I knew it, kids were calling me "Circus Boy." It went on for the entire sixth grade. But I never told Mom.

I swallowed the last corner of sandwich, wishing I had a quart of milk to go with it. Too late now. When it was time to hit the road, Mom didn't stop to shop. She loved traveling at night—said the road was more peaceful with just us and the truckers. But it was always weird to wake up somewhere, on a bus, in a back seat, not knowing if you were going to see desert or pine trees or skyscrapers when you rubbed your eyes.

I moseyed down the hall—that was a word I picked up in Nashville, where everybody was real big on moseying—and peered into Mom's room.

It was packed up tighter than a drum: a whole year's worth of living stuffed into three garbage bags. You'd never know anyone had lived there.

Somewhere inside of them was Mom's secret box. I wasn't supposed to know about it. But once you know something, you can't exactly un-know it.

I was seven when I spotted it in a bureau drawer. It was made out of cardboard, the size of an old-fashioned cigar box, but covered with moons and stars and funny designs. I reached out to touch it, because it was such a pretty box—

*Whoosh!* Mom's hand smacked down on my rear end. "What'd I do?" I remember bawling. "What's the matter, Mommy?"

Her brown eyes bored into me like barrels on a gun. "That's private, Toby. And when something is private, you never, ever open it without permission. Do you understand?"

I understood, all right. But I always wondered what she kept in there. Wherever we moved, there it was, nestled in a bag full of clothes and makeup and silverware, just waiting to be tucked into the back of a bureau drawer or a closet, where I could pretend it didn't exist.

The door to the apartment slammed. A second later, Mom's thongs came slapping down the hall.

"Just wanted to give Johnny a call," she explained. "To let him know we were moving on. And thank him for his generosity."

"Generosity?" I snorted. "You mean the plants? Or the gracious five-fifty an hour he paid you?"

"Money isn't everything," she said. "Believe it or not, that was one of the best jobs I ever had. People are always in a good mood when they're buying flowers. They're usually celebrating something, a promotion, an anniversary, a birthday. . . ."

"A funeral," I put in.

"No, those orders they phone in," she said, missing the point entirely. Or ignoring it. She was glancing around the room, making sure she hadn't left so much as a hairpin.

That was one of Mom's rituals—the Once-Over. Erasing the traces of our existence. Destroying the evidence.

"So what did you do with them?" I asked as she checked under the bed and peered in the closet.

"With what?"

"The *plants*, Mom. Remember? Your little green buddies?"

"I took them down to the Veterans Hospital. I asked the lady at the desk to give them to the patients. Especially the ones who don't get any visitors. You'd be amazed what good company an African violet can be."

"You're right," I said. "I would."

She sighed. "Enough with the sarcasm, Tobe. Those plants *were* my buddies."

Something nagged at me. "The VA? But that's miles away. Don't tell me you dragged those plants on a million buses!"

Mom looked at me mysteriously. "Nope," she said. "I drove."

"We got a car!" We hadn't had a car since the Pinto died the day after we arrived from Nashville. "Where is it?"

"Parked out front. Go see for yourself. Grab those bags and I'll meet you downstairs."

She wanted to finish her Once-Over in peace. I snatched up the plastic luggage and sprinted for the door. "What'd you get? Does it have a radio?"

"Don't get too excited, Junior. It's no Maserati. But the guy at U-Drive Auto Sales said it would get us where we want to go." She pointed out the window. "There's our chariot."

I glanced down at the street. She was right, it was no Maserati—more like a late seventies Plymouth, the size of a tank. But judging by the hood, it had a V-8 engine and power to spare.

"Gee," I said, impressed. "We could fit the sofa bed in the back seat."

Mom laughed. "And here I thought you hated it. You know my rule, Toby: No furniture bigger than a bread box."

I wanted a better look at the car. But at the door, I paused. "You said it would take us where we wanted to go. I just wondered where that was."

"You'll think I'm nuts, Tobe. . . ." She kept the suspense going for a few seconds. Then she said the last thing I expected to hear.

"You can thank me later. But ten minutes from now, we're leaving for Idaho."

*"Idaho?"*

"A little town called Donner, near the Canadian border. Now, scoot. I want to beat rush hour, and we've got some long miles to put in."

Idaho. Potatoes. White supremacists. More potatoes. The train was pulling out of the station, and now it had a destination. Donner, Idaho.

"Okay, Circus Boy," I said under my breath as I dragged the bags down to the metallic-blue hulk. "Head 'em up, move 'em out."

While I stowed the luggage, I admired the speedway lines of our latest wheels. I had already named it the Shark.

I looked back at the Dumpster. In the window I could see Mom moving from room to room, checking to make sure . . .

Of what? I didn't know, and I didn't want to. We were escaping, that's all I cared about.

I turned and hurried up the stairs. I wanted to make sure my skateboard and duffel bag made it on board, before the Donner Express pulled out of town.

The smog was tucked like a quilt over the city as we turned our backs on L.A. I sat next to Mom, staring out the Shark's tinted windows. The front seat was huge, like a big vinyl couch. I propped my feet up on the dash and listened to the engine purr, taking us where we wanted to go.

Sometimes when we traveled I was the navigator, calling out routes from the maps Mom kept under the seat. But mostly I just liked to sit and think.

I didn't think about Phantom. That part of my life was over; and when something's over, I try not to drag it along for the ride. The past is like a garbage chute, as far as I'm concerned. Let it go.

Mom's that way, too. I looked at her as she sat behind the wheel, eyes straight ahead, chin stuck out. "I'm just restless," she once told me, and I believed it. But there were other things that weren't true.

Mary Elizabeth Ryan

The names, for one. Mom never used the same one twice. In Boston she liked to be called Nancy; in Tennessee it was Janine. When she took the florist job, Johnny called her Annette. I knew without her telling me that when other people were around, she wasn't Annie Chase, but this new person: Nancy or Janine or Annette.

"Variety," Mom said. "The world is made to be remade, Tobe, and don't you forget it."

The freeways began to crisscross and tangle as we headed north. When I was little, I thought it was great moving around all the time. Life was one big camping trip, and just being with my mom made me happy. But the last few times, the moves were starting to get to me. Maybe it was that "Circus Boy" stuff. Or maybe it was Mom.

She was older than other kids' moms: over thirty when she had me. That doesn't make me a candidate for some tabloid headline, "Thirty-Year-Old Woman Gives Birth, Amazes Experts!" But sometimes I wondered if that was the reason Mom was so weird.

Like the phone. As in: We never had one. Mom said it cost too much, and besides, who was there to call? All Mom's relatives were dead, she said, and so was my dad; he was killed in a car accident when I was a baby.

Okay, but who doesn't have a phone? Annie and Toby Chase, that's who. And that wasn't all.

We never opened bank accounts—Mom paid the bills with money orders, and she bought groceries with cash. No credit cards—she didn't believe in them. But then you'd see something on TV you'd love to order, and you'd think, oh, right, no phone, no Visa card... forget it!

But pay phones—that was a different story. We'd be at a McDonald's; I'd be gnawing on my burger and Mom would be flipping through the paper. All of a sudden off she'd go, and I'd see her outside at the phone, her back to the street, and she'd stay like that for maybe fifteen minutes. Then she'd come back and sit down like it was nothing.

So then I'd ask her, "Who you calling, Mom?" or "What was that all about?" If we were pulling into a new town, she'd say, "Finding an apartment," or "Checking out a new job." But this past year, when she'd already got an apartment and a job, she'd kick in with the old standby: "You know the rules." In other words, put a lid on it.

As night closed around the highway the headlights began to sparkle past, like a parade. Mom's rules were so much a part of my life, I didn't even think about them half the time. But now that I was older, a lot of them didn't make much sense.

It wasn't that Mom was strict. As long as I didn't break any of the rules, I could pretty much do whatever I wanted: eat pizza for breakfast, you name it. Mom was funny that way—she didn't put restrictions on what I could do, only what I couldn't.

Rule number one: Don't ask questions.

It seemed simple, but it wasn't really. What it meant was, whatever Mom said, you did. Whatever story Mom made up, you went along with it. If Mom told the landlord we were gypsies from outer space, you put a scarf on your head and did your best Martian imitation. If you came home from school and there was a new junker parked in front of the building, you went upstairs and started to pack.

It also meant I couldn't ask Mom about herself. I didn't know where she was born, where she grew up, what happened to her parents. I was born in Denver, Colorado—I knew that much. But how she and my dad got to Denver, how they met, what happened next, was a total mystery.

Number two: Keep your mouth shut. That was a bigger deal when I was little. Mom had to scare the daylights out of me to get me to learn that one. No matter who showed up—the bogeyman, Freddy

Krueger—I was not to say a word. "Even," she said, "if they tell you I'm dead."

Nice thing to hear when you're five years old. But it worked. I was one tight-mouthed little ranger.

Still am, for that matter. But now that I was older, I was onto her—at least about one thing: No one else lived the way we did. No one.

Mom's features were lit up in the green glow of the dash. What's the real story, Mom? I wanted to ask. What's the deal?

Do you work for the CIA? Was I kidnapped? Were my big ears decorating a milk carton somewhere? Sometimes I even fantasized that my dad was still alive and wondering what happened to me. . . .

But I couldn't ask her. Not ever.

That was one rule I made up on my own.

Somewhere along the coast we pulled off the road for a bite to eat. The salami sandwiches had worn off hours ago. I was sleepier than I was hungry, but Mom was wide awake, burning up with the road fever she always got.

I started kidding her about Donner, Idaho. I'd seen a documentary about the Donner Party, a bunch of settlers who got stuck crossing the Sierra

Nevada during a snowstorm, back in the 1800s. They had to eat human flesh to stay alive. It was pretty gruesome, but at one in the morning, sitting in a coffee shop, the idea of a town settled by cannibals cracked me up.

"You gotta watch out for those lawyers in Donner, Mom. I hear they charge an arm and a leg!"

Mom shook her head. "I don't think the Donner Party made it that far, Toby."

"So how did you hear about this place, Mom? I didn't know travel brochures made it that far, either."

"I was reading an article in a magazine at work. It was about vacation homes of the rich and famous. They showed some movie stars' homes up near Donner. And bam—I thought, Toby would really love it up there."

"I would? But I'm not a movie star, Mom."

"Not yet." She smiled, and reached over to brush back my hair. Maybe she figured I already knew a lot about acting.

When the waitress came over, Mom ordered her usual, a cheeseburger and a Coke, and I got a strawberry milk shake. Then Mom got up, saying she'd be right back, and I knew she was heading for the pay phone next to the rest rooms.

I sat fiddling with the salt-and-pepper shakers, looking around at the other midnight ramblers. I was starting to get into travel mode. It felt good to be on our way. Anything was better than what we'd left.

Mom seemed happier, too, when she got back. "Good news, Toby," she said. "I think we can squeeze in a layover in San Francisco on our way up north."

"Great," I answered. "Maybe we can just stay there, and cancel the Donner portion of our fabulous, all-expense-paid vacation."

She tossed a straw wrapper at me. "I thought you'd be happy. Remember when you were a little guy, and we spent that week in the Bay Area? You loved it."

"If you say so." My milk shake came, and I filled my stomach with it. Mom was still talking about San Francisco. "I took a chance and called an old friend. It turns out she'd love to have us stay with her."

"Which old friend is this?" I asked. Not someone we needed to install a phone for, obviously.

I could count on one hand the people Mom knew. There was Fred Hayes, of course. Fred had been a friend of Mom's brother, Martin, who was killed in Vietnam. She and Fred stayed in touch, but it wasn't any kind of regular thing.

That was fine with me. Fred gave me the creeps. Not just because he chain-smoked, and had gray hair and a black beard (which brought to mind two words: shoe polish). But whenever Fred showed up, a few days or a week would go by, and then, like clockwork, Mom would start getting antsy to move.

I didn't know what it was about the guy. But I always put the two things together. I even gave him a name: Bad News Fred.

There were other people, supposedly friends, that we stayed with when we were passing through their town. I remembered a family in South Dakota where we spent Christmas when I was about six or seven. We never saw them again. This was the first I'd heard of anyone in San Francisco.

"Which old friend?" I prodded.

For once Mom didn't slap me with a gag order. "Her name's Carol. We went to college together, a long time ago. She has a place up in Diamond Heights, with plenty of room."

I was starting to feel sleepy, but Mom was wolfing down her food, talking nonstop about Carol, how great it would be to see her again. Finally she stood up. "Let's move out, Chase," she said. "I can feel my second wind coming on. I think if I just keep driving, we can make San Francisco by sunup."

"Great, Mom. Wake me when we get there."

She paid for the meal, and we headed out to the Shark. While she was rearranging stuff to make room for me in the back, a fresh breeze blew in from the ocean. I leaned against the car and took a deep breath of salt air.

"Captain to Navigator. Ready to move out."

"Roger."

I crawled into the back seat and curled up. Now that I wasn't five, sleeping in the car was a tight squeeze. But as soon as the Shark swung back on the highway, my eyes closed, and my mind began to seesaw.

For the first time in months I fell into a deep, dreamless space. No trains careening through the Twilight Zone. Just the ocean breeze coming in the window while my mother steered us through the night.

A hand reaches for me. It grows bigger and bigger, covering my mouth. I can't breathe. I'm scared to look, but I have to open my eyes—I have no choice—so I open them and . . .

The plastic seat was wet where I'd pressed my mouth. I groaned and sat up. Tan street signs with black lettering floated past the Shark's windows.

"We in Frisco yet, Mom?" I asked, resting my chin against the seat.

"You're better than an odometer," said Mom. "We just pulled into the city limits a few minutes ago. We should be at Carol's soon."

We stopped at a light. Mom glanced back at me. "God, Toby, you look like you just fell out of a tree!"

"Feel that way, too." I rubbed my cramped legs.

"Well, hang in there. You can wash up at Carol's while she and I catch up on old times."

The Shark labored up the famous hills of San Francisco until we reached the top of Diamond Heights. We parked on a steep street in front of a Victorian house.

While Mom went to investigate, I got out and stretched my legs. From here you could see the whole city, spread out like a corny postcard. It was about seven in the morning, and the streets were cold with mist.

Mom was climbing a flight of steps, checking to make sure she had the right address. Just then the door opened, and a woman about Mom's age stepped outside.

"Annie?" she said.

She'd called her Annie—not Jane, or Nanette, or Brunhilda. Maybe they really were old college pals.

I squinted at the house and dug my hands in my pockets while Mom and Carol hugged and squeaked and fussed.

Then Mom turned and beckoned me forward. "And this," she said, "is my pride and joy. Carol, my son, Toby."

I cringed at the "pride and joy" stuff and headed up the stairs, my duffel slung over my back.

"Hello, Toby," the woman said warmly. "Come right inside. Annie, let me fix you up with some coffee, and then I'll take Toby up to his room."

Before I knew it, my bag was stowed in a big white room, and a stack of towels was shoved in my arms. With a wave—"Come downstairs when you're ready for breakfast"—Carol closed the door. I didn't need a hint. I peeled off my clothes, jumped in the old claw-foot tub, and turned on the shower full blast.

Once I was dressed, I realized how hungry I was. Following the smell of coffee drifting up the stairs, I headed down the hall.

There were doors on either side of the hallway, but only one was open. It was a cool home office, with a computer and a fax machine.

I walked over to the computer. It was huge, with speakers and a CD-ROM drive; nothing like the beat-up PCs they'd had at school. I wondered if Carol had any computer games she'd let me try.

Then I saw something taped onto the side of the computer. My mouth went dry as I leaned forward to look. It was a picture of my mom.

But not just any picture. It was Mom when she was young—barely out of her teens. She had long, dark hair; her head was thrown back, and she was laughing at the camera. I couldn't believe she'd ever been that young.

I couldn't take my eyes off the photograph. I didn't have any pictures of my mother. That was another rule Mom had—no camera, no snapshots.

As I gazed at Mom's face, I felt a familiar itching in my fingers. I thought of all the stuff I'd ever taken. Some I kept, stashed in the chess set hidden in my duffel bag. Most of it I tossed, or left behind when we moved, like that trail of bread crumbs in *Hansel and Gretel.* It was just something I did. I'd been doing it for years.

Toby was here. Maybe that's all it meant.

I unpeeled the tape holding the picture to the monitor and slipped the snapshot in my pocket. Behind me, the fax machine suddenly whirred to life.

Mom and Carol were at the kitchen table, dishes and coffee cups scattered in front of them. They looked up and smiled at me as I came into the room.

"Eggs, pancakes, or both?" Carol offered. She laughed when I nodded. A few minutes later I was digging into a giant stack of blueberry pancakes, heavy on the syrup, eggs over easy, orange juice, bacon.

"Teenage boys," Carol said. "I have a son, too," she told me. "Jeff starts college in the fall.

He used to eat me out of house and home."

"Where is he?" I asked. It might be cool to have someone to check out San Francisco with.

"He lives with his dad in Marin," Carol said. "Now, how about seconds on pancakes?"

No argument from me. When breakfast was over, I put my dishes in the sink and went upstairs. The fax machine was still spitting out pages. It must be a pretty long document. I walked over to see what it was.

"Can I help you find something, Toby?"

Carol stood in the door, a questioning smile on her face.

"I was just looking at your computer." I leaned over as if I was checking out something on the screen. My hand reached in my pocket and pulled out the picture of Mom. With my back to Carol, I stuck the photograph onto the monitor.

"Are you into computers?" Carol asked, coming into the room to stand next to me. I searched for a hint of accusation in her voice, but there wasn't one—just polite interest, like a friendly librarian helping you find a book.

"Kind of. We got to use them at my last school. I mean, the one before that. . . ."

"I guess you move around a lot. Your mom was telling me all the neat places you guys have lived."

While she was talking, Carol reached past me for the stack of pages lying in the fax tray. She slipped them into a drawer.

"Yeah, I guess so." I wanted to get out of there so badly, I could taste it. But Carol was still pinning me with her friendly smile.

So I zapped her.

"Mom said you were roommates or something, back at UCLA, huh?" I was improvising—fishing, actually.

"No, not UCLA." Her smile didn't falter. But it didn't matter. The part of me that knew how to read people had just picked up a blip on the screen. *She doesn't know how much I know,* came the readout. *She isn't sure what to tell me.*

"I thought that's where you guys met. At school," I said. "Mom said you were in college together."

"Actually," Carol said, "it was high school." She pointed to the photograph. "That's where this picture was taken. I dug it out when Annie called to say you were coming. Weren't we young, though!" She laughed.

We both gazed at the picture while I absorbed another piece of information.

One thing about Mom's training, you learn to pay attention. You learn to listen. And I knew

Mom hadn't said anything about high school.

Carol was lying.

I looked at Carol, at the shiny computer screen flooded with colors, the sunny room full of office equipment and filing cabinets. For the first time I wondered what we were doing here.

"Hey, listen, that was a great breakfast," I said, backing out the door. "Your son's a lucky guy. Wish I could eat that great every day. I'd be a linebacker by now!"

My babble-o-meter was stuck at full throttle, but Carol didn't seem to notice. She was nodding her head and smiling. I kept going. I didn't stop until I had reached the shiny, quiet hallway.

I sped down the hall and into the bedroom. Then I flopped down on the neat, white bed. My stomach was churning, and not just from too many pancakes. I wondered if Carol would tell Mom she'd caught me in her office.

Finally I heard her footsteps move down the hall and descend the stairs. I counted to a hundred. Then I slipped off the bed and out the door.

The picture was just where I'd left it. Mom's face grinned at me trustingly as my fingers closed around the photograph.

A cold mist hung over the Bay when we pulled out of San Francisco. I carried our stuff down to the car. While Carol and Mom said good-bye, I waited in the front seat, looking at the maps.

It had been a good stopover. Sleep, showers, plenty of food. During the day I took the bus to the waterfront and saw some of the sights. At night we sat around and watched videos.

But the whole weekend, I couldn't shake the weird feeling that Mom and Carol had never met before Saturday. I caught myself watching them the way you'd watch a play, to see if they were getting their lines right.

I watched them make popcorn and clean up the kitchen together, the way old friends are supposed to do, just picking right up where they'd left off. Not nervous or careful or shy.

Maybe that was the problem. It was too good.

But what about the picture in the office? If

Carol had never met Mom before, what was she doing with her picture?

There wasn't any answer.

I asked Mom what Carol did, why she had that office upstairs. "She's a union organizer," Mom answered. "You should ask Carol to tell you about it."

But I never did.

Now I sat in the car and watched the two women hug on the front steps. Like I said, it was a good rest stop. But it wasn't until Mom got in the Shark, gave the horn a blast, and started the engine that I could finally take a deep breath.

Things were back to normal.

The wheel bearings burned out the day after we left San Francisco. Other than that, and the fact that the Shark had a broken radio, it was a pretty good trip.

Even so, it took three and a half days to get to Idaho, counting auto repairs. I'll say one thing for Mom's approach to finances—cash definitely talks. We were in and out of that garage so fast, the mechanic barely had time to stuff the bills in his pocket.

We drove north and east, pulling off at picnic areas shadowed by redwoods for a few hours' sleep, then back on the road. By the time we reached eastern Oregon, I was getting pretty sick of truck-stop chili and counting license plates.

"Guess who I am."

It was Mom's favorite travel game. I wasn't really in the mood for it—I hadn't been for about five years—but as usual, I gave in.

You got twenty tries to read her mind. Fat chance: Mom always won. Still, it was the only time she let me ask her questions.

"You're a person?"

"Uh-huh."

"Dead person?" She nodded.

That really narrowed it down.

By the time I determined that she was a dead guy who didn't live in America or start World War II, my interest had definitely waned.

"I'm turning all the cards over, Mom. You're . . . Genghis Khan!"

"Very close," she said. "Christopher Columbus."

"No fair! You said you didn't live in America."

"Didn't you ever study the explorers? Columbus never set foot on the mainland. Okay, your turn."

Payback time. I decided I was a brain-dead mutant from outer space. Major wipeout. We called it a draw, and I settled back with my headphones for the long haul.

Even without a radio, Mom was humming under her breath as we crossed the Idaho state line.

"Look, Toby." She pointed at the acres of farmland that stretched into the distance.

I pulled off my headphones.

"What do you suppose they're growing?" I asked. "Could it be . . . potatoes?"

"Nothing wrong with spuds."

I squinted out the window. "Gee, look—I think I see Bruce Willis riding on a tractor over in that field. No, wait—it's Clint Eastwood, plowing the north forty!"

Mom rolled her eyes. "Very funny," she said. "But just wait until we get to Donner. No potato fields up there. Just clear, beautiful lakes and gorgeous mountain scenery."

She went back to humming as we passed through the outskirts of Boise. As I watched the fields and houses tick by, a tough question began to form in my head. By the time it reached my lips, it was too late. I'd already blurted it out.

"So, did Carol ever meet Dad?"

The humming stopped. Long pause. But when she finally answered, Mom's voice was calm. "Your dad? No, sweetie, that was years after I left school. Why do you ask?"

"Just wondered," I said.

We didn't talk about my father much. It wasn't a rule, exactly; more like a mutual agreement, that things were a lot more pleasant if you didn't bring him up.

But, since I'd already stepped into the quicksand, I decided to jump in all the way. "So, like, were you guys married?"

Total silence. Late afternoon sunshine splashed through the windows, making Mom squint as she stared at the road. I kept my eyes straight ahead.

The silence went on for about five miles. She's mad, I decided, risking a glance at my mother's rigid profile. She's mad, and I'm the world's biggest idiot, and I'll never, ever—

"God, you were a nice baby."

Her voice sounded so close to tears, I was amazed to see that she was not crying. "Just so chubby and calm and happy," she went on, "like a little Buddha. That's what Jack—your dad—called you when you were born. Bodhi. Short for bodhisattva."

"Body *what?*"

"Bodhisattva. It means one whose essence is enlightenment."

"It does, huh? Well, I'm sure glad you settled for Toby," I said, to cover up my shock. "It, uh, means one whose essence is ninety percent water."

Mom's eyes softened. "It does, huh?"

Without warning, she swerved the Shark into the parking lot of a roadside restaurant. It was a road rally move: My seat belt practically cut me in two. Then she turned to face me.

"Just this once, I'm going to answer your questions. Yes, I was married to your father. Not the most traditional wedding—a Buddhist ceremony on a Hawaiian beach at sunset. But legal, nonetheless. I loved him so much, Toby, I guess it's hard for me to talk about. Because he's gone now, and I miss him."

What can you say? Nothing. I nodded my head, feeling like a fool.

"And I'll tell you this, while we're at it. You look more like him every day. There. Now, let's go eat. I'm starving."

So we went inside, and Mom ordered her cheeseburger, and I got my shake. But the whole time I was trying to picture my mother and some guy with blue eyes and big ears standing on a beach, wearing Buddhist leis.

But at least she'd let me ask, just this once, a personal question.

Which might not sound like a big deal to most people. But when your essence is enlightenment, something approaching a fact can practically make your day.

In Boise, Mom stopped and bought me a book about Idaho. Since I didn't care much about the subject, I wasn't sure why she'd bothered. But it gave me something to look at, while we made our way up the state.

Judging by the map in the book, there were maybe five towns in the whole state of Idaho. The rest of it was state parks, national parks, historical parks, and bird refuges, with some major rivers and canyons thrown in between the potato fields.

After a while, though, I started to get into it.

"Hey, Mom, check out this picture. Do you think there are bears up in Donner?"

"You mean just wandering the streets? I hope not!"

"Can we spend the night at Seven Devils Mountain? It's up near Hells Canyon."

She shrugged. "Why not, if there's a campground."

As the sun set—a big Technicolor production, worthy of a special effects Oscar—we drove along the Snake River, then found a place to set up camp for the night. Pines and rocky cliffs bordered the purple sky. Any minute I expected to see a giant grizzly shouldering its way into the clearing.

Someone had left the makings for a fire in the cookout grill. I scouted around for dry twigs and leaves, and after a few false starts, got the fire going. I opened the cans of stew we'd bought in Boise and set them over the grill.

After dinner, Mom pulled the sleeping bag out of the Shark. As the flames crackled, we spread it on the ground and stretched out to watch the fire.

"Tomorrow we make Donner." Mom rested her chin on her hand. I watched the light from the flames flicker across her face.

"If it's anything like this, I'm ready!"

She twisted her head to look at me. "It's better, Tobe. It's going to be better than any place we've ever lived. I can just smell it."

"No, that's skunk," I said, as a sharp, critterish odor rose in the air, mingling with the smoke from the fire.

After a while the fire died out, and we brushed off the sleeping bag and settled in the car for the night. I didn't want to end up some Idaho mountain lion's midnight snack.

I stretched out in the back seat and listened to Mom settle into sleep. After a minute I heard her breathing deepen and then soften into a tiny snore.

I flipped onto my back so I could look out the window. There wasn't much to see—a few stars, some pine shadows spreading over the car. Not like the darkness in L.A., the dead flip-side of day-time, when things were halfway real.

I rolled up my jacket and shoved it under my head for a pillow. Maybe Mom was right this time. Maybe this move really was the end of the trail.

First, though, we had to get to Donner.

"Toby?"

Her voice startled me.

"Turn off your brain and go to sleep."

"Yes, ma'am."

"G'night, my little Bodhi," Mom said.

**6**

We were supposed to hit Donner by midafternoon. Only we couldn't find it.

"Did you take the Foster Lake turnoff?" I asked Mom after we'd driven for miles with nothing in sight. I held up the map and stared at the tiny speck of Donner, at the top of the long, craggy wedge that was Idaho.

"Of course I did. It's the only exit this far north."

I peered at some red and blue squiggles. "Here's something called Forest Road 102."

Mom looked exasperated. "I don't think the town of Donner is inside a forest, Toby."

"Wait, here's a road!" I pointed at one of the squiggles.

"That's a river," Mom said. She sounded fed up.

"Well, don't blame me!" I said.

Mom's voice was grim. "We'll just have to ask someone, I guess."

I huddled by the window and stared out at the forest on either side of the road. Mom hardly ever stopped to ask for directions. Things must be desperate.

Besides, I didn't want to point out the obvious: There was no one to ask.

By five o'clock the shadows were starting to climb down from the mountains and cross the road. It was definitely time for Plan B, if there was one.

"Let's just keep going a little farther," I suggested. "This road must lead somewhere."

Mom was scanning the horizon. "I don't know, Toby. Maybe we should go back to the highway and—"

That's when I saw it. It wasn't much of a sign; green letters on a thick piece of pine, it nearly blended into the trees next to the two-lane blacktop.

"Mom," I said. "Back there."

"What?"

"You wanted to ask someone for directions. Here's your chance."

She spun the Shark into a big U-turn and aimed toward the sign. It was propped next to a muddy turnoff that led into a clearing. Next to the dirt road, a split-log fence disappeared into the trees.

"'Sam's Nursery,'" Mom read.

"Let's just ask directions and get it over with," I said. I clutched the map as if a big arrow that said "Donner" might jump up and hit me between the eyes.

Mom pulled onto the dirt road. We bumped along for a short distance. Around a turn, the road abruptly ended.

"This must be the place," Mom said. She switched off the motor. We got out and stood in front of Sam's Nursery.

Outside a big, sprawling greenhouse, potted trees and bushes were lined up in neat rows. Off to the left was a trellised yard with more plants laid out on big covered tables. There was no one in sight.

"They must be closed," Mom said. "Now what?"

I'd run out of things to say. I looked up at the snowcapped peaks in the distance. Then I spotted something. A gray, shingled farmhouse sat on a small hill behind the greenhouse. A battered blue truck was parked next to the sagging porch.

"Check it out," I said. "Whoever owns this place

must live here, Mom. I mean, wherever Donner is, I bet it's a commute."

"Good scout, Toby." Mom looked relieved. "Let's see if anyone's home." We started past the nursery, up the path toward the farmhouse.

"You folks lost?" The voice seemed to come out of nowhere.

Something moved in the shadows of the trellis, and a man came toward us. He had a shovel in one hand and a cowboy hat in the other. Resting the shovel against one of the bedding tables, he gestured toward the Shark. "Saw the plates," he said. "Figured you were a little early for the Christmas tree season." His face split in a grin as he put the hat on his head.

"We're not tourists," Mom said. "But you're right, we're lost."

The man was sizing us up, his eyes sliding from Mom to me and back again. He sees something he trusts in Mom, I thought. He's not so sure about me. . . .

"We're trying to get to Donner," Mom explained. "My son found it on our map, but I must have taken a wrong turn."

"Nope. The only wrong turn you could make was about twenty miles back, and that one would take you clear up into Canada. Donner's another ten miles along Indian Falls Road," he added, pointing toward the blacktop. "If you had kept going, you'd have run smack into it."

"Told you," I muttered, but Mom ignored me. Her eyes were taking in the well-stocked bank of plants, the trees with their balled-up roots, the cool depths of the greenhouse.

"You must be Sam," she said. And that was all. But from the way she said it, I knew she was saying a lot of other things.

Here we go again, I thought. This guy was going to give in, just the way Johnny had at the florist shop. Mom was about to cast her spell.

The man seemed to sense it, too, because he shifted his feet a little, digging one toe in the dirt.

"Like the sign says, this here's my nursery. Well, part of it. The tree farm's back of the house."

"My name's Jenny Parker, and this here is Toby." Mom was picking up on the local accent, like she always did. It was a pretty convincing twang.

Jenny Parker. I stored the name away for safe-keeping.

"So what brings you up this way?" Sam asked.

Now that we knew Donner was within spitting distance, I was ready to hit the road. But Mom wasn't. Instead, she walked over to the bedding table and picked up one of the plants. She held it for a moment, felt the leaves.

"Seems a little chilly to leave the aspidistra out," she remarked. "Especially when you have that conservatory back there."

I had to hand it to her. She wasn't exactly subtle, but Sam was starting to pay attention.

"I move them in at night," he said. He paused and pushed back his hat. "You know something about plants?"

"As a matter of fact, I do." Mom held up her fingers and wiggled them at Sam. "Ten thumbs, all green," she added.

"You need a job." Not a question this time. His eyes took in our shabby car crammed with plastic bags, the map clutched in my hand, Mom's tired face.

She was looking at me. It's your life, my look said: Go for it. I'd be a fool not to, Mom's eyes answered. I'll give it my best shot.

She turned to Sam. "I've never worked in a greenhouse before," Mom said, "but I know a lot about plants. I'm better with ornamentals and exotics than garden perennials." Her voice was steady, but she spoke in a rush.

The man stood with his hands in his back pockets.

"I had a boy working for me," he said abruptly, "but he took off to Glacier for the tourist season. So I'm kind of in a bind."

He nodded at the nursery. "Can't pay much, you understand."

Mom was nodding, too, keeping time with Sam. As I watched her head move up and down, I hoped he didn't see the desperation in her eyes.

"But the job comes with lodging, for you and your son."

Mom's eyes began to shine. "You mean, a place to live? For free?"

"It's not much of a place, Mrs. Parker. A cabin, really. Some folks might even call it a shed. But it's warm enough when the sun goes down, and there's running water."

"Running water!" Mom pulled her sweater around her. "Mister, you just said the magic word."

Sam smiled, shaking his head. He'd just gotten his first blast of the Annie Chase whammy, and I could tell he wasn't sure what to make of it. When my mother wants something, she doesn't take no for an answer. Or even a maybe.

"Tell you what," he said. "I'll show you folks the cabin. You're welcome to spend the night, see what you think. I won't hold it against you if you decide to try your luck somewhere else."

He headed toward the back of the nursery, with Mom at his heels. "Donner's a funny little town," he remarked. "I don't quite know what someone from the outside would see in it. Or in this place, for that matter."

I folded the map of Idaho and stuck it in my back pocket. Good old Sam might not realize it, but we weren't going anywhere. The minute she'd seen this place, Mom had staked her claim. It didn't even matter if all that stuff Mom had said about exotics and ornamentals was one big pile of horse manure.

For better or worse, we were home.

The cabin was pretty basic. Sam must have built it himself, I figured as I looked around. The walls were rough, hardly more than planks; the heating unit turned out to be a Franklin stove at one end of the room.

One room. Just when I thought I'd escaped from sofa bed hell . . . here we go again.

Mom was looking around, too. "This looks real comfortable, Sam." She was starting to remind me of the Purty Schoolmarm out of some old Western.

"The bathroom's back here," Sam said, pushing aside a curtain to reveal the toilet and the tin box of a shower. "I could put a door on it for you," he offered, "if you decide to stay."

Gosh, that's right generous of you, Mister Sam, I thought while he pointed out the kitchen: a linoleum counter, a sink, some shelves, and a hot plate.

I cleared my throat. "I don't suppose there's a pizza delivery place in Donner?"

"No, you'd have to go all the way to Copper City if you want pizza," Sam said. "But you're welcome to use the kitchen up at the house for meals."

I choked back a laugh. If Sam expected Mom to do any cooking, he was in for a big shock. But she was already thanking him in her homespun twang.

Sam adjusted his hat. "Well, this is it. If you need anything, come up to the house. The back door's always open." With another flick of his brim, he left.

As soon as he was gone, Mom spun around. "Toby! Don't you just love it?" She whirled around the room in crazy circles until she lost her balance and flopped down on the sagging bed in the corner.

A thick cloud of dust flew up. Mom choked, coughed, and began to laugh.

I sat down on a wooden chair that matched the rickety table in the middle of the room. "Mom," I said while she was catching her breath, "if this were a tree house or a fort, and we were eight years old, I'd be out of my mind with joy. But do you really want to stay here?"

"Why not? It's shelter, it's free, and it comes with a job attached. Right now, Toby, I'd settle for a pup tent. But this place has got some real possibilities."

The bed gave another dusty wheeze as she propped herself on one elbow. "Besides, don't you think Sam seems nice?"

"He's okay," I said, tracing the initials that someone had burned into the tabletop.

"Come on, Toby. Didn't I tell you our luck would change? Give it a chance."

I didn't like it, but it didn't make any difference. Mom's rules didn't give me veto power. Besides, it wasn't going to be permanent.

"Just do me one favor," I said.

"You got it."

"Stop with the stupid accent, like you're Miss Kitty on *Gunsmoke*."

"Was I doing it again?"

"Just like in Nashville. Only worse."

She looked repentant. "I'll try not to," she said.

"And another thing."

She sighed. "What?"

"Don't bring any dumb plants in here, okay?" I stood up. "I'll get the luggage. You figure out where I'm supposed to sleep."

"I think we'll both take sleeping bags for tonight," she said. "In the morning I'll ask Sam about getting a bed in here for you. And some kind of partition."

"Something in brick would be nice," I said, not quite loud enough for her to hear.

"You know something? I don't even know Sam's last name. I forgot to ask."

"You mean, you *plumb* forgot," I told her. But Mom was already scoping out the cabin. I had to admit, she looked like she belonged here already.

I wasn't sure if I did. But at least we had a place to spend the night.

"Look," she called, "the hot plate works! Dig out the rest of those groceries we bought in Boise," she added as I headed out the door. "I can heat up some of that stew."

The sun was setting in earnest when I got outside; it left a pinkish-orange glow on the snow-capped mountains in the distance. I stood next to the Shark while the darkening pines closed in around the nursery. L.A. was long gone now, and so was Carol, with her computer and her fax machine and her phony stories about Mom.

After an uncomfortable night on the cabin floor, Mom and I took showers and headed up to the farmhouse. Though the sun was barely up, there were lights on in the kitchen. Sam sat at the table reading, a pair of glasses propped on his nose. He looked up when Mom tapped on the door.

"Morning," he said. "How did you like the cabin?"

"Just fine," Mom answered. "I hope you don't mind, but I put the mattress outside in the sun. It could use a little . . . airing."

Sam nodded. I was dying for a cup of the coffee steaming on the stove, but Mom was still negotiating.

"And we'll have to find something for Toby to sleep on. Is there a store nearby?"

Sam rubbed his chin. "Don't worry, we'll find something," he said. "In the meantime, Edgar and I were just going over some seed catalogs. You might want to take a look at them, Mrs. Parker."

"Call me Jenny. I'm sorry—I didn't catch the rest of your name, Sam."

"It's Wilder," he said. "Now, how do you like your eggs?"

"Scrambled," I said. "Who's Edgar?"

Sam pointed under the table. I looked down. A thick yellow tail gave a thump. A second later, Edgar poked his big Labrador head out and gave me a black-lipped grin. When he got to his feet, he practically took the table with him.

"Wow," I said, stroking Edgar's powerful back. "That's a major dog."

"Canadian Lab," Sam said. "They're bigger than a standard. Good hunter," he added as he broke some eggs into a bowl and began to beat them into a yellow froth.

A few hours later, we got our first look at Donner.

I knew it had to be Donner because there was nothing else in sight, except for the mountain range looming behind it. Donner was basically one street. There was a gas station at one end, and some low brick buildings at the other that Sam said were government offices.

"Right there you can take your driving test, talk to the sheriff, and buy a stamp under the same roof."

"How convenient," Mom observed.

"Only they test your eyes before they'll sell you the stamps," I said.

Mom laughed, but Sam didn't. Or maybe he didn't get it, I thought.

Between the jail and the gas station was a general store that doubled as the bus depot, a diner called May's Grill, and an auto parts and farm equipment outlet. And that was basically the sum total of Donner.

We bounced along, squeezed in the front of Sam's truck, while Edgar swayed on all fours in the back. Mom tried to talk him out of it, but Sam insisted on giving us the grand tour. I kept looking for the movie stars' houses that Mom had talked about, but all I saw were trees, some small ranches with big satellite dishes out front, and a few cows and horses.

Finally Sam stopped and pointed to a squat brick building set back among the trees.

"That's the high school," he said.

I stared at the homemade banner draped across the front of the school. GO REBELS, it said. BEAT FOREST LAKE!

Mom nudged me. I groped for something positive to say. "We're the Rebels?" I asked.

"Basketball team," Sam said. "Not much of a record," he remarked as we pulled away from the school.

I laughed. I was starting to like the way Sam said things. Terse, but he made his point.

While we drove around, I noticed something else: Sam liked Mom. A couple of times I saw him glance at her while she exclaimed about this or that, and when she looked back at him, his eyes blinked a lot.

"Where's the nearest mall?" I asked as the truck swung back on the main road. "We don't have to get a real bed. I mean, I wouldn't mind a futon or something like that."

"What do you think, Sam?" Mom asked. "There must be a department store you could take us to."

"If you don't mind a day's drive."

A day's drive? Just to buy some tapes, or ride the escalators? I nudged Mom. "Go Rebels," I said under my breath.

Back on the main street, Sam pulled up in front of the square government building.

"Just got an idea," he said. "I'll be right back."

While we waited for Sam, I got out of the truck and walked around back to visit Edgar. He stood up when he saw me and gave his thick tail a workout.

"Hey there, buddy," I said, offering him my hand to lick. "What do you say you and me go scare up a squirrel or two, huh, Edgar? Would you like that, boy?"

Edgar thought that was a great idea. I was still discussing it with him when the double doors to the post office/jail/license bureau swung open. I watched Sam and a tall man in a tan uniform wrestle a huge mattress through the doors and out to the truck.

"Heads up, Edgar!" Sam called as he heaved the mattress into the bed of the pickup. Edgar scrambled out of the way.

"Toby, I'd like you to meet Sheriff Hal Springer. He's graciously agreed to let you borrow a mattress from his jail."

"It's hardly been used," the sheriff said. "We haven't got much of a crime wave here in Donner. I'd let you have the frame, too, but I'm afraid they're bolted into the cells."

Sam turned and shook the sheriff's hand. "Much obliged, Hal."

"Sure thing, Sam. Glad to hear you've finally got some help around the place." The sheriff walked up and stuck his head in the cab of the truck.

"Pleased to meet you, ma'am," he said. "Sam tells me you're fixing to stay up here. Stop by anytime, and I'll show you around."

I couldn't hear what Mom said. I watched the sheriff nod and tip his hat, then stroll back toward his office.

I ran a hand over the mattress. It was practically brand new, twice as thick as the sofa bed we'd left at the Dumpster.

"I guess some prisoner will have to sleep on the floor," I told Sam as we climbed back in the truck.

"I wouldn't worry about it. If Hal runs out of room—why, he'll just have to send 'em up to the nursery to bunk with you."

It was Sam's idea of a joke, so I smiled. I turned to Mom. "So how do you like my new bed? Fresh from Cell Block One."

I must have said something wrong. Mom's face was dead white. Her eyes looked strange, and a big crease stood out in the middle of her forehead.

"Mom? You okay?"

She drew a hand over her eyes. "Just a touch of dizziness. Must be the altitude catching up with me."

Sam looked concerned.

"Altitude sickness is no joke, Mrs. Parker. People who aren't used to these mountains can get as sick as the devil with it."

Mom nodded. Her hands were trembling.

"Put your head down if you feel dizzy," he told her, "and take some deep breaths. We'll have you back to the house in no time."

He started the truck, and we flew out of town, taking the bumps in the road two at a time. Mom's head was down, and she was breathing slowly in and out. All of a sudden I felt worried, too.

Mom had been fine the night we'd spent in

Hells Canyon, and on the drive up to Donner. I didn't know what was wrong, but I was sure of one thing: Whatever made her sick had nothing to do with the altitude.

Nothing at all.

I keep thinking I'll get used to the changes. Different towns, different Mom; different everything. Just when you figure out what you're supposed to be doing, something comes along to take its place.

Then again, getting used to something isn't the same as trusting it.

The second day, I was still getting used to life at Sam's Nursery. In the morning we climbed the path to the house. Mom and Sam went over the day's schedule while I had coffee and fooled around with Edgar. Then I hung out at the nursery. Mom was still learning the ropes. I sat on the potting bench and checked out the people who came by. Some of them bought plants, but mostly they wanted advice from Sam.

I watched old ranchers pull up in beat-up

trucks to ask why the cattle weren't eating their feed, or what to do about a vegetable patch the wife had planted. Sure enough, Sam always had an answer.

He'd studied agriculture at college, he told me, while I followed him around the greenhouse. That surprised me: Sam didn't seem like the college type. He was too quiet and slow. If you told him a joke, it took him all day to get the punch line. I couldn't picture him sitting in a lecture hall with his hand in the air.

Then again, maybe he had the answers back then, too.

In the afternoon I headed up into the hills that rimmed the tree farm. I found a spot to sit and watch what was going on in the woods.

If you sat still long enough, a few deer would venture out from the trees, and you'd hold your breath, in case they heard something or smelled your scent. The minute they did, their tails would give a flip: danger! And off they'd go, with only a quivering leaf to show they'd been there.

Climbing higher, I found a huge, flat rock perfect for sunning. I lay on my back and stared up at the wide blue sky. An eagle sailed past, and I watched the way it flew, like a fist opening and closing, clenching and releasing in perfect time until it caught a tailwind. Then it opened its powerful wings and soared away, sliding down a long, invisible chute.

I looked down at my hand. Slowly I clenched it, then opened it, stretching my fingers wide. That must be how flying felt, I thought, watching the eagle become smaller and smaller as it swooped back up, suspended in the mountain air.

When I got back, Mom was staring at the hot plate.

"We're out of stew," she announced.

I flopped down on her bed. "Why didn't you say something? I could have brought back some wild game. Spotted three bear, a cougar, and a moose. Good eatin', I bet."

"Very funny," Mom said.

"Hey, I did see a deer," I told her. She ignored me.

"Didn't Sam say you could get pizza in Copper City? That's only a three-hour drive."

"Forget it, Toby," Mom said. "You get cleaned up, and then we'll go work something out with Sam."

The kitchen windows were steamed up when we reached the house. Sam opened the door, and I saw a big pot of water boiling on the stove. He smiled when he saw Mom.

"I was just about to invite you two for supper," he said. "How does spaghetti sound?"

Mom paused at the door. "Actually, that's what we came up here to talk about."

The smell of garlic and tomatoes was killing me. I glanced at Mom. What was there to talk about? I was starving, and there was food. End of discussion.

"The truth is, I'm not much of a cook. Toby and I usually eat out a lot, but there's no place around here to go. So . . . "

"So have dinner with me," Sam said.

Mom and Sam were having some kind of showdown with their eyes. I couldn't tell what they were saying, but it wasn't about spaghetti.

I remembered how she was with Johnny, the florist. He was old and fat and married, but it was the same thing. Mom always knew how to get what she needed, whether it was a job or a meal or a bunch of stupid plants. She knew how to work people, especially guys.

Some of them knew it and some of them didn't. Some of them didn't care. Some of them even seemed to like it.

I looked back at Sam, and wondered which kind he was. And if he was really as slow as he'd seemed.

Sam put down his spoon and wiped his hands. "Jenny," he said, "it would be a pleasure to have someone to cook for. But if you feel uncomfortable about it, I'll deduct the money for meals from your pay. Sound fair?"

"Fine," Mom said. "But only if you let Toby and me clean up the kitchen."

Sam glanced at the spattered counters and shrugged. "Looks like you picked the right night," he said. "Toby, grab a plate. I hope you like garlic. It's home grown."

I didn't wait for Mom to up the ante. I grabbed a plate and headed for the pot of pasta.

I had seconds and thirds. Sam was a good cook. But he wasn't as slow as I'd thought.

He started off easy. "Where you from, Jenny?" he asked, and then hopped up to grab the garlic bread out of the oven. Mom was coiling spaghetti on her fork, but I could tell the wheels were turning. I chewed, waiting to see what she'd say.

"Texas, originally," Mom answered.

"No kidding? Texas?" Sam brought the bread back to the table and handed me a hunk. It was hot and delicious.

Then he looked at Mom. "Funny," he said. "Most folks from Texas have pretty distinctive accents. Sounds like you lost yours along the way."

"You're thinking of west Texas," Mom said smoothly, reaching past me for a slice of bread. "My people come from Austin. My father taught at the university there."

Sam smiled. "Now, see? I knew there was a reason. A professor? What did he teach?"

"English literature," Mom told him. "His specialty was eighteenth-century poetry."

Even though I'd seen her do this a hundred times, it still amazed me. It was like watching a good magician pull the old coin out of the ear. It might be a corny trick, but in the hands of a master, it could still take your breath away.

Here's the thing about Mom. She's not just making this stuff up—she *knows* it inside out. I'd never heard her mention Texas or eighteenth-century poetry. But ask her a question about either one, and she could wipe the floor with you, and teach you a few things about armadillos and John Donne while she was at it.

Sam didn't try. But he didn't give up, either.

"So where's your dad, Toby?" he asked, spooning sauce over his pasta. "He's not going to show up at the nursery one fine day, is he?"

"Toby's father is dead," Mom said. "He was killed in a car accident before Toby was born."

It bothered me when she said that. I knew she

was just going with the flow, saying whatever sounded real, but I wished she'd leave my dad out of it.

Sam looked bothered, too. "I'm sorry," he said. "I didn't mean to sound flippant."

Mom shook her head. "Don't apologize. Still," she added, "it's been rough on us. Especially Toby. My parents died a few years ago, and that was pretty much it, as far as family goes. So," she smiled at Sam, "now we're hobos."

Sam winced. "Sounds grim. I hope you don't mean that, Jenny."

I felt a little sorry for Sam. Don't worry, I thought—she doesn't.

I inhaled the last strand of spaghetti and wiped my mouth. "Where's Edgar?"

Sam began to clear the plates. "Outside, chasing the ghosts away," he said. "Now, how about some coffee? I usually take a cup after a big meal." He paused. "Or do you think it would keep you up?"

"No, coffee's great," Mom said. She got up and headed for the sink. "I'll wash, Toby. You can dry."

We did the dishes and Sam made coffee. As he and Mom were sitting down to drink it, I started for the door.

"I think I'll turn in," I said. "Hey, thanks a lot for the spaghetti. It was great."

"Don't mention it," Sam said. "Sleep well, Toby."

When I got to the door, I looked back at Mom, sitting at the table with her coffee mug, waiting to fill Sam's head with mythical stories of her childhood.

Just like she had at Carol's, I thought. Except Carol already seemed to know them.

Did Sam? The thought made me feel cold. I began to go back over the trip, over the road to Donner. Was it an accident Mom had found a job so quickly?

It *had* to be. We were lost, right? There was no way Mom could have found this place unless I'd noticed that sign.

Mom looked up. "Forget something?"

I eased away from the door. "No, it's nothing, Mom. G'night."

"G'night, kid. Leave the light on. I'll be down soon."

I moved off into the twilight. Sure enough, there was Edgar at the foot of the steps, his golden coat pale against the shadows. He came up and sniffed me, then gave me his doggy grin.

"How ya doing, fella? Can't put one past you,

can we? I bet you can smell trouble a mile away."

I patted him and then made my way down the dark path to the cabin.

Sam had rigged up an old curtain around my bed. I holed up behind it and tried to read. When that didn't work, I rolled over and watched a beetle tiptoe on its pronged feet across the floor. I wondered what Mom was telling Sam. Sometimes it took some fancy footwork to keep up with her stories. I pictured Sam, the shy way he smiled at Mom. I wondered why it bothered me.

It didn't bother me when she told Johnny we were transplanted New Yorkers, how we'd left Queens after her divorce. It hadn't bothered me all the times before.

The beetle was still teetering toward me. Without a thought I brought my book down on top of it.

After a while I lifted up the book and took the dead beetle outside, where some hungry spider could put it to good use. I was about to go back inside when I looked up the hill and saw Mom step out onto Sam's porch. The light over the door caught the copper highlights in her hair; they formed a brief halo around her head.

Sam came out, too, and they stood talking. After a moment, Mom started down the steps.

Mary Elizabeth Ryan

Then I saw her pause and walk back to Sam.

Right then my stomach did a double jackknife off the high board. I don't have infrared vision, but I know a good-night kiss when I see one. And whether I liked it or not, that's exactly what it was.

A few days later, I told Mom I needed a ride into town.

"I want to get some stuff to take up in the hills. A pack, a compass . . . some binoculars, maybe, for eagle spotting. They must sell hiking stuff at that general store."

She was unloading bedding plants from the back of Sam's truck. "I'd take you, Tobe. But we've got our hands full right now. How about tomorrow?"

I paused. "I could take the Shark."

"You're fifteen. You don't even have a learner's permit."

I didn't give up. "Maybe I could walk."

Mom set the plants down and wiped her face. "Maybe you couldn't." She gave an exaggerated sigh. "It's ten miles into town, at least. And don't even think about hitchhiking, Toby."

I shrugged. "Maybe I could run it," I said.

Mom ignored me. I watched her write some stuff on her clipboard. After a moment, I went back to the cabin.

I pulled out my duffel bag and felt around for the box with my chess set. Placing it on the bed, I opened the box.

Under the folded chessboard was all the stuff I'd swiped over the years. Most of it was junk— motel ashtrays, ballpoint pens, a dead Zippo lighter—plus a few treasures: a silver mirror I'd taken off a teacher's desk; a watch some guy had left on a rest-room sink; a pair of sunglasses that belonged to a girl I'd liked.

And the picture of Mom I'd taken from Carol's office.

There was some money in there, too. I pulled out a twenty and stuck it in my pocket.

Then I put the box away, shoved my Dodgers cap on backwards, and set off for town.

About a mile down the road, a guy in a pickup motioned me into the back of the truck. Swaying on a tarp next to an ancient lawn mower, I rode into Donner.

It didn't look any different—as quiet as a tomb. I wandered along the main street, peering into the windows of the auto parts store.

When I got to the general store, there was a sign on the door. CLOSED FOR LUNCH, it said.

I peered across the street at May's Grill. It didn't look very inviting. I kept on walking.

I was starting to wish I'd eaten before I'd left. I trudged past the post office/jail, trying not to think about the long, hungry walk back home. Then I smelled something.

Food.

At first I figured it must be lunchtime for the inmates. Then I saw a little storefront tucked at the end of the block. A small, hand-lettered sign hung over the door: Good News Café. On the window someone had painted in big, shaky letters: HOT FOOD. ALL YOU CAN EAT.

That was good enough for me. I pushed open the door.

A string of temple bells jingled from the doorknob as I stepped inside. The Good News Café reminded me of every Asian deli I'd seen in L.A.: a bare room crammed with tables and chairs, a row of booths along the back. A weird assortment of posters was taped up on the walls: the Grateful Dead, the Pope, the New York Yankees.

Except for me, the place was empty. Then I noticed a girl sitting behind the cash register by the door. She was reading a fashion magazine and chewing gum. As I stood there, a pink membrane of gum suddenly erupted from her mouth, obscuring her face.

When it finally collapsed and she'd gathered it back with her tongue, I walked over to the register.

"Hi," I said. "You open?"

She looked up. I could tell she wasn't glad to be there. She squinted at me from behind small, wire-rimmed glasses and slowly put down her magazine. "Are you from around here?" she asked. "I haven't seen you before."

Friendly, I thought. "Yeah," I said. "I'm from around here. As of a couple days ago." I paused. "Are *you* from around here?"

The girl's eyes narrowed further. "My dad's from Cambodia," she said. "But I'm from around here."

Reluctantly she closed the page of fashions and got up. "Sit anywhere," she commanded. "I'll get you a menu."

I picked a table near the front and took off my cap. The girl handed me a plastic card. "The special's teriyaki," she said.

I studied the menu while she stood there waiting. "I'm Sunny," she said suddenly. "That's my name, not the weather report."

Her glasses twitched up her nose. Something

close to a smile crossed her face. "I know, dumb name, huh?"

"It's okay," I said. "I'm Toby."

Sunny's head moved up and down. I figured she was going to stand there until I ordered something, so I pointed at a number on the card. "Is Combo Number Three any good?"

Sunny shrugged. "I can't recommend it," she said. "The special's teriyaki."

"I know, you told me that. What's wrong with Combo Number Three?"

"My mom hasn't made it yet. So, you want the teriyaki? It's pretty good."

I sighed. "Do I have a choice? Okay, I'll take it." Sunny bobbed her head and vanished. A moment later she came back with a pot of tea and set it down in front of me.

"Are you going to Valley High?" she asked while I poured the tea. "When spring break is over?"

She was wearing boys' pants about three sizes too big, and a flannel shirt. I wondered why someone who looked like that would read about fashions in a magazine. Then again, what did I know about girls? Or fashion, for that matter.

"I guess so," I said. "Anything I should know?"

Sunny pulled up a chair and parked herself.

"It's boring," she said, drawing out the word for emphasis. One hand sneaked up and gave the glasses a nudge. "We moved here from Seattle three years ago. I hate it," she added.

"Seems okay to me," I said, just to keep her talking. I liked the blunt, odd way she said things. "What's wrong with it?"

"No boys," she said. "Asian ones, I mean. The kind my parents like. I have a little brother, but he doesn't count."

"Obviously."

"All our relatives live in Calgary. We go up there on holidays. But it's pretty boring there, too. Where did you move from?"

I thought about it. Longer than I should have. Sunny's eyes were flicking over my face, drawing conclusions. I could hear her strange, clipped voice delivering a report to Sheriff Springer after I left. "He was weird. I didn't like him. You should check him out."

"Texas," I said, after a long sip of tea.

"Do you know how to ride a horse?"

Good question: one I hadn't thought of. "We lived in Austin," I said, wondering where the hell that was. "Near the university," I added. "Not many horses around there."

Her flannel shoulders twitched. "Too bad."

Someone in the back called her name. Sunny got up and shuffled off toward the kitchen, her long pants dragging on the floor.

She was arranging the food in front of me when the temple bells jingled again. A man came in and stood at the register near the door.

"How's it going," he called to Sunny. I looked up, and my mouth went dry. It was Sheriff Springer.

He saw me, too, and gave me a wave. "Hey, there," he called. "How's that mattress working out?"

"Great," I said. I didn't really feel like talking about my jailhouse bed with Sunny listening. But I didn't have much choice. The sheriff was hitching up his belt and coming over to my table.

"Don't let me interrupt your meal," he said. I gripped my chopsticks. The teriyaki smelled sweet and strong. But the sheriff didn't seem in a big hurry to leave.

He gestured to Sunny. "Say, how about bringing me the same?" She nodded and went off to the kitchen.

Sheriff Springer turned back to me. "Mind if I join you?"

Yes, I did mind. I was officially AWOL, my lunch just showed up, I was starving, and something about Sheriff Springer gave me the creeps. You bet I minded.

I looked up at the sheriff. "Sure. No problem."

He sat down and waited for Sunny to bring the tea. Then the sheriff poured a cup and remarked, "How's your mom getting along?" He glanced around the café, as though he expected to see her. "She and Sam doing some shopping in town?"

I took a bite of rice and meat, chewed and swallowed. "Uh, no, actually, they're not. I . . . walked."

"Walked!" Sheriff Springer laughed. "That's quite a hike. You hear that, Sunny? Toby here walked into town from Sam's place."

He watched me eat for a while. Then he asked in his low Idaho drawl, "Do much fishing?"

"Fishing?"

Sheriff Springer sipped his tea and nodded at me. "There's some fantastic fishing around here. Mostly cutthroat or bass. I take the boys up to Indian River every chance I get. Tell you what," he said. "I'll ask Sam to cut you loose some afternoon, and we'll find you some waders."

I paused. I wasn't sure what a cutthroat was. I definitely knew I didn't know how to catch one. But I nodded.

"Sure thing," I said.

When the sheriff's lunch arrived, I went over to the cash register where Sunny was bent over her magazine.

"Listen," I said, "that was great. But I'd better be going."

She looked up at me and then over at the sheriff. "How come? You didn't even finish your food." Her nose wrinkled, and she scratched it. "Did you really walk all the way up Indian Falls Road?"

"I was bored," I said. I picked up the check and went back to the table to retrieve my cap. "Nice to see you again, Sheriff. I'll definitely take you up on that fishing. But it's time for me to hit the road."

Sheriff Springer frowned. "Don't be silly. You just sit tight, and I'll run you back to Sam's."

"No, really, I've got stuff to do. . . ." I reached in my back pocket for the twenty.

My hand came up empty. I pictured the bill lying under the tarp in that guy's truck, where it must have fallen out.

Sheriff Springer was watching me intently. I felt the blood rush to my face as I dug through my other pockets. They were empty, too.

The sheriff paused. Then he set down his

chopsticks. Slowly he reached over and pulled out a chair.

"Like I said, you just sit tight. And don't worry about the check," he added. "It's happened to all of us. Hey, Sunny," he called, waving to her, "you want to bring Toby his fortune cookie? He'll be staying for a bit."

On the ride back to the nursery, Sheriff Springer kept up a steady stream of questions.

I sat in the front of the van looking out the window. Even though he hadn't put me in back behind the grill, I still felt like a prisoner.

"Sam said you folks moved up here from California. Is that right?"

When I nodded, the sheriff chuckled.

"Now, what in the world could have brought you all the way up here?"

I couldn't tell whether he was curious or just making conversation. Either way, I figured it would be safer to answer.

"My mom read about Donner in a magazine. She thought it looked like a neat place to live." It sounded lame as soon as I said it. But it was the truth, wasn't it?

"A magazine, huh? What do you know—we're famous!"

Sheriff Springer's ruddy face was fixed in a permanent grin. But somehow I got the feeling he didn't believe a word I said.

The van bounced along Indian Falls Road while the sheriff asked how we'd met Sam. He marveled at how lucky we were that Sam needed help at the nursery, and then asked what grade I was in at school. When I said tenth, Sheriff Springer nodded.

"Great. Valley High can use a tall kid like you." He began to ponder the Rebels' chances of making it to the state finals before I could point out that team sports weren't my specialty. At a couple of schools I'd thought of trying out, but Mom put her foot down. Too competitive, Toby. Big waste of time, Toby. I'm too busy to take you to practice, Toby. Anyway, by the end of the season we were usually gone.

I was glad when the van pulled off the road and parked in front of the nursery. Sheriff Springer glanced at the plants lined up in front of the greenhouse. "Sam and I are old friends, you know. We used to come out here a lot when my boys were little. When Sam's wife and kid were still around."

"No kidding?" I said. "Sam has a family?"

Sheriff Springer glanced at me. "Had," he

said. "He doesn't mention them much. Can't exactly blame him."

I wanted to ask why. But the sheriff was peering through the windshield. "Say, isn't that your mother? Why, I believe it is."

Mom was pushing a wheelbarrow around the corner. Her eyes widened when she saw the county emblem on the door. Then her jaw tensed as Sheriff Springer got out and ambled over to her.

"Afternoon, ma'am. Got an express delivery for you."

As I climbed out of the van I saw the worry line cross Mom's forehead. She set down the wheelbarrow and gave the sheriff a careful grin.

"It can't be another mattress," she said, "so you must mean my son."

"Bumped into Toby in town. Thought I'd save him a walk home."

The sheriff pushed back his hat and adjusted his gun belt. I could tell it was something he'd done many times before. "Now, ma'am, just speaking as a parent, I don't think it's a good idea to let Toby walk Indian Falls Road. It's not safe for pedestrians. These good old boys around here drive pretty fast. I should know—I've clocked them myself." He laughed at his own joke.

Mom nodded. "Of course, Sheriff. I'm so

sorry Toby inconvenienced you." She shot me a stern glance.

"No trouble at all, Mrs. Parker," he said. "Say, is the owner around? As long as I'm here, I might as well stop in and say howdy."

"Sam's up at the house," Mom said.

The sheriff touched his wide-brimmed hat. Then he shook a finger at me. "Stay out of trouble, Toby. And talk to Coach Saunders about a tryout with the Rebels. Tell him I sent you."

"Will do," I said. We watched the sheriff stroll around the corner and head up the hill.

The minute he was gone, Mom jerked around to face me. Her eyes were blazing. "I want to talk to you. Now!"

The door to the greenhouse clicked shut behind us. Mom's face was pale and grim.

"You are never to go into town without permission, Toby," she said.

"But Mom—"

"When I saw the sheriff pull up in that van, I didn't know what to think." For a moment she stood there, one hand on either side of her face, as if there was something she didn't want to see. "I want to trust you, Toby. But you're making it tough."

"It wasn't that big a deal...."

"Anyone could have seen you in that county van. This is a small town. People talk."

You never cared where I went before, I thought. But I didn't say anything. Mom ran a distracted hand through her hair. I watched her pace up and down the aisle of plants.

"I want us to fit in here, Tobe. I'm asking you not to blow it."

"Does that mean we're staying? For more than a couple of minutes?"

We eyed each other like opponents in a boxing ring.

"I'd like to," Mom said finally.

"Because of Sam?"

An odd, assessing look crossed her face. "Is that what this is about, Toby? You're jealous of Sam?"

I thought about the kiss I'd seen on the porch. Mom's private life was her own business, always had been. There had been guys in the picture before, but I'd learned not to make them a part of our lives. Our lives always moved on, and they stayed behind. Which was fine with me.

But Sam seemed different. This whole move seemed different.

"I don't want to pretend we're from Texas," I told her, to get off the subject of Sam. "It's the one place we've never lived. Why did you have to pick Texas?"

Mom shrugged. "Because it's the one place we've never lived." She picked up her gardening gloves and shoved them in her back pocket. "Look, I didn't mean to unload on you like that. Still friends?"

I nodded.

"No more unscheduled trips into town, Toby. Do you promise?"

I nodded some more.

"And what did the sheriff mean about trying out for the Rebels?"

"It was just a joke," I said.

The door to the greenhouse opened, and Sam stuck his head in.

"Hey, Tex," he called. "Got a Single Early back there for Hal? He needs something to brighten up his office."

"I'll get you one." Mom went over to the table of flowering bulbs. She picked up a bright red tulip and plopped it in my hands. "Give this to the sheriff," she said. "And make sure you thank him for the ride."

"Sure thing—Tex."

I walked out to the parking lot where Sam and the sheriff stood talking next to the van.

"Well, look at that!" the sheriff exclaimed as I gave him the potted flower. "Looks good enough to eat, doesn't it?"

"I'd try some salt and pepper," I said. "The Single Earlies are a little bland."

The sheriff laughed so hard, I thought he'd pop a blood vessel. "Funny kid," he said, shaking his head.

"Thanks again for the ride," I said, in case Mom was listening. "I'll pay you back for the lunch."

He waved it off. "Already taken care of," he said.

Sheriff Springer climbed into the van and set the tulip on the dash. "Think about what I said, Sam," he called as he started the engine.

Sam nodded and waved. We watched the van back out of the parking strip, spin around, and then head back the way it had come.

"What does he want you to think about?" I asked.

Sam rocked back on his heels. "Hal and his family are big on trout fishing. He's organizing a trip over to the Indian River on Sunday. Thought you might like to come along."

"Do I have a choice?" I said.

Sam gazed at me for a moment. "You are a funny kid, aren't you."

"I don't know how to fish," I said. "But I've seen people do it on TV. I thought it looked kind of boring."

"Didn't your mom ever take you fishing back in Texas?"

I glanced around. Mom was coming out of the gardening shed with another wheelbarrow of seedlings.

"Like I said, I don't know how to fish."

Sam shrugged. "No harm meant. But I'd be glad to show you how it's done. It might not be as boring as you think. Besides," he added, clapping me on the back, "we wouldn't want to hurt Hal's feelings, would we?"

"Nope," I said. "We sure wouldn't."

At dinner, Sam told Mom about the fishing trip.

"Sam says it's fun," I told her.

"Nothing better than panfried trout," Sam announced. "And the best part, Tex, is that you get to clean 'em!"

I caught on before Mom did. We both laughed at her horrified expression. But when I got up to clear the dinner dishes, I kind of wished Sam would stop calling Mom Tex.

The joke's on you, it seemed to say. Or even: I know you're both a couple of liars, but I like you anyway. Deep down I didn't think that was what Sam meant. But I couldn't be sure.

I swished the dishes around in the sudsy water while Sam set up the coffee for the morning. Edgar was snoozing under the table. Outside it was dark and cold, but inside the kitchen there was a warm, good feeling. The way people got together for a meal—not saying much, just settling in for the night. A normal, relaxed feeling.

I wasn't used to that feeling. I didn't trust it. I couldn't imagine it lasting. Soon enough, something would happen, and the cozy kitchen would vanish, and off we'd go, like always.

"How about a hand of pinochle?" Sam said.

Mom snickered. "Pinochle? I didn't know people really played that game. I thought it was just something they had in old Westerns."

A slow smile crossed Sam's face. He was charmed. "Well, I guess that makes me an old Westerner," he said.

He sat down at the table across from Mom. "Toby," he called, "why don't you go in my desk and get the pinochle deck? They're in the second drawer."

"Sure," I said. I wiped my hands on the dish towel and walked into the living room.

There was an old mahogany desk in the corner

where Sam did his accounts. I stared at the contents—calculator, pencils, a small framed picture of a woman and a little boy. A stack of bills held in place with a magnifying glass.

I picked it up. It was small, with an ornate handle, carved in the shape of a mallard duck.

I heard Mom's high-pitched laugh, the rumble of Sam's reply. "Hurry up with those cards, Toby," Mom called. "I've got someone here who doesn't think I can beat him at pinochle."

I reached in the drawer and found the deck. Right before I left the room, I stuck the magnifying glass in my shirt.

Toby was here.

Early on Sunday morning, Sam was waiting in his truck. I rubbed the sleep out of my eyes as I climbed in. "Where's Edgar?"

"I don't take Edgar fishing," Sam said. "He'd rather hunt. Besides, we've got to leave your mom some company, right?"

As we drove up to the lake, I tried to feel excited about the fishing trip with Sheriff Springer. I wanted to like it, for Sam's sake. My coming along seemed to matter to him; I wasn't sure why. Did he feel sorry for me? Or was it something else—a family thing, maybe?

Sam turned the radio to a country station, oldies. Merle Haggard began singing about Bakersfield. I thought about Sam's wife and kid, about what might have happened to them. Did they just leave—disappear one day, like Mom and I had done so many times, without a forwarding address? Without a word?

As dawn colored the sky above the highway, I ran through all the places we'd left. The people were still there, back in St. Louis and Boston and L.A.—Mom's bosses, my teachers, the kids in my class. No one ever knew we were going to leave, and we never said good-bye. One minute we were there, and the next minute—poof. Gone.

I wondered if any of them missed us. It never occurred to me to miss them. What was the point?

When you don't say good-bye, it's like you were never there. Like you didn't exist.

Maybe, I thought, that was the point.

We turned off the main road to where a sign said Indian River Campground. Sam looked over at me. "Still awake there, Parker?"

"More or less."

"You don't sound awfully enthusiastic. But you're going to catch a fish today if it kills you."

I looked back at Sam. "Death threats? Whoa, I'm starting to get enthusiastic now."

We had gone a few miles before I asked, "What happened to them?"

"Who?"

"Your family. Sheriff Springer told me they weren't around anymore."

Sam didn't answer, but I saw him stiffen. Sam's face was rigid. Just tell me it's none of my business,

I thought. I'll shut up, apologize, whatever. Just tell me to take a hike.

But it was too late. Sam was Sam. I had asked, and now he felt obligated to tell me.

"My wife and son were killed in an accident two years ago," he said after a long pause.

He didn't elaborate. The truck bumped along. Dwight Yoakum sang about Cadillacs. At the next bend, a glint of water showed through the trees.

"I used to take my son, Mark, fishing up here," Sam said as we pulled into the campground. "Guess I figured it was something a kid would enjoy. I didn't mean to twist your arm, Toby."

I was starting to feel guilty. After all, he just wanted me to have a good time.

"So do you bring your own worms on these expeditions?" I asked. "Or do we use fake ones?"

"They're called flies," Sam said. "Don't worry, I've got a box full."

As the sun crept over the mountains, Sam parked the truck on the banks of the Indian River. It spread out before us, cold and flat, a sluggish length of metallic gray. It made me shiver to look at it.

Thwack! A red down vest fell across my lap. Sam reached behind the driver's seat and tossed me a pair of gloves. "There's a thermos of coffee under your seat. It's cold on the river until the sun comes up."

Reluctantly I shoved my arms into the vest. Cold was not my idea of a good time. When you've slept in your clothes in the back seat of a car for as many years as I have, or on an unheated bus, cold is not something you look forward to.

Sam jumped down from the truck and stood gazing at the river. The chill in the air didn't seem to bother him. "Great, isn't it?" he called.

"Quiet, you'll wake the fish!"

I turned to see a Jeep Cherokee pull up alongside the truck. Sheriff Springer stuck his head out of the window. "What did you do, Wilder? Take an illegal shortcut?"

Without waiting for an answer, he unhooked his seat belt and climbed out. Behind him I saw two male shapes get out, too, and start unpacking their gear.

"Toby! Great to see you, son," the sheriff boomed. "Guys, this is the boy I was telling you about. Walked into town all the way from Sam's."

I pictured the sheriff telling every person in Donner about my great feat. And it wasn't even true.

"This is my son, Andy, and his cousin Rob," he was saying. "They're on break from Boise State.

Anything you need to know about trout fishing, just ask them. Been doing it since they were big enough to hold a rod."

Andy and Rob barely glanced at me. They continued hoisting their tackle boxes and clothes out of the Jeep.

I stood next to the truck, wondering what I was supposed to do. Everyone was moving in a different direction. I felt like climbing back in the truck and going to sleep.

"Toby, over here. I want to show you something."

I went over to the bank. Sam was fixing a feathered hook onto the end of a fishing rod. He handed me the rod and showed me how to cast. I tried it a couple of times, dipping the hook in and out of the water, reeling the line back in and throwing it out again. It was harder than it looked.

"You'll get the hang of it," Sam kept saying. I watched him pay out his line, dropping it precisely into the deepest part of the river, letting it drift to where the fish spread circles in the water. He made it look easy. When I tried it, my own line sank like a stone a few feet from the bank.

After many more attempts, Sam sent me up to the truck to get the coffee. I climbed inside and closed the door. As I sat there rubbing my freezing hands, Sheriff Springer's face appeared in the window.

"Don't tell me you've given up?" he asked.

"Trying to get the feeling back in my hands."

"You need a better pair of gloves," he chuckled. "Tell you what. You go over to my Jeep and find yourself a decent pair. Gore-Tex lined. I buy them down in Boise."

"Thanks," I said.

"The back's open," the sheriff called as I trudged toward the Jeep. "Help yourself."

I opened the tailgate. The Jeep was stuffed with gear. Sure enough, a pile of gloves was stacked neatly in a box.

I reached for a pair and then paused. Next to the gloves lay a pair of binoculars. Small, powerful, and expensive.

As I stared at the binoculars, I felt the stealing trance slip over me like a tight, smooth skin. Take me, they seemed to say. I'm yours now.

My heart sped up, but I felt in control. That's how it feels when you're actually taking things—like you're invisible, powerful, entitled.

I picked up the binoculars. They fit snugly into the pocket of the down vest.

"All set?" the sheriff's voice boomed behind me.

I froze, my hand stuffed in my pocket. Slowly I took it out and picked up the pair of gloves.

"Maybe you'll have better luck wearing those," he said, and clapped me on the back.

I nodded. Waving the gloves at Sheriff Springer, I went back to the truck and grabbed the thermos of coffee. I carried it down to the bank where Sam was hauling in his second fish.

"Sheriff gave me these gloves," I told Sam, holding up my hands. "Said they'd bring me luck."

"Just take your time, Toby," Sam said. "If you're patient, the right fish will find you."

After what seemed like hours, I drew a tug on my line. My heart practically stopped

"I've got something, Sam!"

Sam put down his rod and came over. "Let him have it, Toby. Give him all he wants. He won't get away."

The sound of the line releasing sizzled in the cold air. At the other end, the fish felt heavy and insistent. The line continued to unreel until I was sure it would break. Sam stood next to me, calling out encouragements.

"Let him tire himself out. You'll know when he's had enough."

I could feel the invisible fish straining at

the line. He didn't seem tired in the least.

"Try pulling him in," Sam told me as the taut line disappeared under the water. "Back and forth, go with his movement. That's it. Let him get himself caught."

I spun the reel as hard as I could. Suddenly the fish came flapping out of the water, its silver scales gleaming. I let out a yell and nearly dropped the rod.

"Whoa! He's a monster, Toby." Sam was pounding me on the back while I struggled to haul in the trout. When we finally got him onshore, I saw Sam was right. The fish was enormous.

"Can I keep him as a pet? I'll name him Moby Dick!"

Sam grinned. "The only thing we're calling this fish is dinner."

At noon we stopped and ate sandwiches that the sheriff's wife had packed. The others had caught a few trout, but nothing the size of old Moby.

"Didn't I tell you those gloves would bring you luck?" Sheriff Springer said as he got up to admire my catch.

"Not so, Hal," Sam said. "What we have here is plain, old-fashioned beginner's luck. Remember when Don got that rainbow? That thing looked like a barracuda!"

Hal chuckled. "He was experimenting with bait. What was he using that day? Hershey's Kisses?"

He picked up another sandwich and turned to me. "We're talking about my brother, Toby. Don was a legend in these parts. Until the war came along."

"Come on, Dad," Andy said. "Don't go into that."

"I'm just talking to Toby here." The sheriff took a drink from the thermos and wiped his mouth. His smile was gone. "This place was red, white, and blue in those days. Not many guys from here got drafted; they enlisted. I spent my hitch supplying ships in San Diego. My baby brother went over the border to Canada because he refused to go to Vietnam. My folks wrote him off as a draft dodger. Even after he came back during the amnesty in the seventies, they never spoke to him again."

"I had an uncle who was killed in Vietnam," I said into the silence that followed. "I never met him, though. I mean, I wasn't around then or anything."

The sheriff studied me intently. "Which

branch of the service? Do you know?"

"My mom doesn't talk about him much," I said, starting to feel nervous.

As if he could sense it, Sheriff Springer homed in on me. "Sam was saying your ma's people were from Texas," he went on. "That's by way of California, huh?"

I tore off a piece of my sandwich and tossed it in the river, just to watch it sink. This whole conversation had gotten a long way from trout.

"We've moved around a lot," I said.

Sheriff Springer shook his head. "Never understood that life myself," he said. "When you're from Donner, you stay put. Except for military service and college, we all come back. Right, Sam?"

He suddenly glanced up over the top of my head. "Hey, Andy! Was that a bear up there? Through those trees?"

We all turned to look.

Andy shrugged. "I didn't see anything, Dad."

"Run up to the Jeep and get me the binoculars, son. If there's bear in these campgrounds, Fish and Game will want to know about it."

The sandwich turned to sawdust in my mouth. I fixed my gaze across the river at the invisible bear while Andy sprinted up the bank. I didn't know what to do. I didn't feel powerful now. Just stupid and caught. Like the fish in the river.

A moment later he was back. "Here you go, Dad."

I looked up and saw Andy hand the sheriff a big black case. I felt dizzy with relief. Slowly I picked up my sandwich. The sheriff was training his high-powered lenses across the river, shaking his head. "Could have sworn I saw that critter."

He looked over at me and grinned. "Of course, I've been known to have a powerful imagination," he said.

We drove back to Donner, a bucket of silver fish swaying in the back of the truck. I kept thinking of them back there. I wondered if fish felt anything, whether they knew they were somewhere they didn't belong.

We stopped to buy gas. While Sam was filling the tank, I went inside the mini-mart and studied the rack of candy bars. My hand closed around the binoculars. I wondered if Hal had seen me take them. I was pretty sure he hadn't, but just thinking about it made my heart beat fast.

"Hungry?"

"No, but I'll take one anyway."

"Sweet tooth, huh?" Sam took the Snickers bar

I held out and went to pay for the candy. He bought us each a cup of coffee, too, and we went back out to the truck.

I ate the candy bar in three bites. Sam sipped his coffee while he recorded mileage in a notebook he kept on the dash. Everything Sam did was precise, orderly, useful. I liked it, but it worried me. I couldn't picture Sam dealing with the unexpected, with danger or chaos.

In fact, I couldn't picture what Sam was doing with Mom and me in his life at all.

That night Sam fixed the trout, panfried, just like he'd promised. He cleaned them himself. Mom and I laughed and ducked as the guts sailed past us into the compost bin.

"Good for the plants," Sam said. "Fish is great fertilizer."

"I knew that," Mom said, and she gave him a nudge.

It was late when she came back to the cabin. I was pretending to be asleep.

"What time is it?" I asked.

"Hush," Mom said. "Go back to sleep."

"What were you doing? Talking about fertilizer?"

"Pretty much. Good night, Toby."

"G'night."

Two days later, the last day of spring break, Sam dropped us off at Valley Regional High so I could register for school. I waited on a bench outside the office while Mom went in and had "a little talk" about my transfer records.

I leafed through an old issue of the *Reader's Digest* while Mom did her routine. From the time it took, I knew it wasn't just a little talk—more like a big song and dance, an entire b.s. production number. I wasn't sure it would fly. My grades and attendance at Fillmore had both been miserable.

But it must have worked. When she came out, the lady behind the counter was smiling at me. I was officially enrolled.

While we waited for Sam, I asked Mom how she'd fixed it to get me into school. "You didn't bring any of my transcripts, right?"

Mom gave a mysterious shrug. "Let's just say I know the right things to say."

"What are they?" I persisted.

"What difference does it make, Toby?"

"I just wondered."

"You've never been kept out of a school yet," Mom said. End of subject.

An activities board hung on the wall near the entrance. I walked over and studied the list of clubs and meetings.

"Look, Mom," I said. "They've got a wildlife club. Says they go on hikes and stuff. Might even see a mountain lion. That would be pretty cool."

Mom looked over my shoulder at the board. "I didn't think you were into clubs," she said.

I waited for her to tell me clubs were a big waste of time, that she wouldn't be able to pick me up after school, that there probably weren't any mountain lions around Donner.

But Mom just nodded. "Seems like a pretty nice school. I'm glad we left Los Angeles, aren't you?"

I nodded.

"Things are going to be different this time, Toby," Mom said, and she really seemed to mean it.

I heard a noise. I looked up and saw Sam's truck rattle off the main road.

I followed Mom out to the curb and waited for the truck to pull up. Sam swung the passenger door open.

"All set?" he asked.

"Piece of cake," Mom said, all smiles.

The next day, a yellow school bus stopped in front of the nursery and took me to school. The minute I got to my first class, I knew Mom was wrong. It wasn't going to be different. The reason was Henry Hatcher.

Mr. Hatcher taught social studies. Except he

liked to call it history. "Nothing social about it, gang," he said the first day of class. "If schools were honest, they'd call history anti-social studies, because it's mostly a long series of wars. Nothing social about it."

Mr. Hatcher wasn't very sociable himself. He had a limp and a scowl and almost no hair. He barked when he talked. Mostly he loved talking about war, and you could tell he relished all the gory details. Right away I decided he didn't scare me.

Halfway through Mr. Hatcher's Top Ten List of blood and gore, I felt a poke in the back. I looked around and saw glasses, black hair, a pair of teasing eyes.

"Psst!" Sunny said. "What happened?"

"What do you mean?"

"Figured the sheriff arrested you," she said. Her foot thudded against the seat of my chair. "'Cause you couldn't pay for your teriyaki."

I grabbed her foot and glared at her. Sunny let out a yelp. Then I saw her eyes drift past me. I looked up, too. Hatcher had stopped lecturing. He was walking over to me.

Here we go, I thought. Joe Friday all over again. I could hardly wait to start skipping class.

"You," he said, pointing at my desk. "What's your name?"

"Don't you mean my serial number?" I said. There was a smattering of laughter.

Mr. Hatcher peered at me for a moment. "According to the seating chart, your name is Toby Parker."

"So if you knew my name already, why did you ask?"

Up close, I could see that his face was covered with smooth red welts, like burns. Mr. Hatcher didn't have any eyebrows.

It made me feel funny when I noticed that. But I didn't look away.

He leaned so close, I could smell the salami sandwich he'd had for breakfast.

"Mr. Parker, do me a favor. Go easy on me in this class."

"Go easy on *you*?"

"That's right. I don't have the patience of a saint, and I don't like smart guys disrupting my class."

I stared down at my desk. The room got very quiet.

"Tell you guys a story," he said, turning to the class. "When I was a little older than you, I got drafted. I did two years overseas. A lot of nightmares happened over there; some of them happened to me." He made a gesture that took in his lame leg, his bald face, the shiny network of red scars.

Hatcher turned back to me. "The point, Mr. Parker, is that sometimes I'm not in a very good mood. So if you can check your attitude at the door, I'd appreciate it."

No one giggled. I shifted in my seat.

"Here's the deal. Every kid in my class has to do a research project on American history. Next week, when I hand out assignments, you're getting the toughest one I give."

"What is it?" I asked.

"The Vietnam War. Think you can handle it, Parker?"

"Sure," I said quickly. "I mean—yeah, I'd like to do it."

The bell rang. Nobody moved.

"One more thing," Mr. Hatcher barked. "Miss Thieu, you'll be working with Mr. Parker. Got that?"

If Sunny had a problem with it, she was telling it to the top of her desk.

"Okay. I want these projects to be more than facts and figures. Talk to people. Talk to your parents—believe it or not, they're people, too."

Groans, some giggles. Hatcher's face relaxed. "History isn't just the past. We're all part of it, and it's part of us. So make it real. Okay, at ease."

Mr. Hatcher sat down and began marking attendance sheets. "See you in class," he said as each kid filed out.

Sunny drooped past me, clutching her books to her flannel chest. I wondered if she felt punished, getting stuck with the hardest project in the class. Getting stuck with me.

I picked up my books and headed for the door.

"Parker?"

I turned back.

"For your information, a soldier doesn't supply his serial number to a member of his own platoon."

What could I say? "Yes, sir."

Henry Hatcher paused. "Unless you're suggesting that I'm the enemy?"

I looked him in the face, took in the welts, the scars, the beady blue eyes. "Not yet," I said.

He chuckled. "Isn't it always the way? The smart guy's a smart kid. Go figure." Hatcher shook his head.

"Huh?"

"Beat it, Parker. I'll see you in class."

Sheriff Springer must have talked to the coach. He came up to me after P.E., to ask if I'd ever played basketball.

I looked at Coach Saunders's eager face. The

last time we'd ever stayed anywhere for an entire season was L.A., and my mind sure wasn't on basketball. Even if we were here next winter, I was no sports star, no team player.

I pictured running laps, whistles blowing in my ear, lectures on team spirit and winning attitudes. Getting pissed off at Coach Saunders. Not showing up for practice, getting kicked off the team . . .

"Sorry," I said. "I have to work after school."

He looked disappointed. "Let me know if you change your mind," he said. "I'm already scouting for next year."

"Right," I said, gathering up my books. "Next year."

Sunny caught up with me while I stood out front waiting for the bus. "Hey," she said, poking me with her sharp elbow. "What did you think of Hatcher?"

"He's one strange unit," I said.

"Definitely," she agreed. She paused. "Sorry I got you in trouble." She peered up at me. "You mad?"

"No, I'm not mad."

She heaved an exaggerated sigh. "Good," she said. "I hate it when people get mad for no reason. Like my parents!"

Jab.

"No offense," I said, "but if you don't want to make people mad, maybe you shouldn't kick them and poke them."

As my bus pulled up I watched her shuffle away, her oversized pants swimming around her legs. Basically nice. Relentless, kind of strange, but not a phony. Nothing phony about old Sunny.

"Hey!" I called. I let out a piercing whistle. Half the kids waiting for buses turned around, but I didn't care. "You busy on the weekend? Maybe we should get together and talk about this project."

Sunny nodded. "I work on Saturdays. At the café." She paused. "But it's usually not very busy."

"Maybe I'll see you there."

I got on the bus and found a seat in the back. As the bus chugged up Indian Falls Road, I thought about school—how it was different from the one in L.A. in some ways, and the same old story in other ways. The ones that had to do with me, anyway.

I still had my doubts about Hatcher. There was definitely something spooky about him. The way he stuck his face out like a weapon, daring you to look him in the eye and count his scars.

But he wasn't a Boyer, who talked the talk but didn't really want to know. Mr. Hatcher wasn't a phony, either.

And when it came to nightmares, I was pretty sure Mr. Hatcher knew about those, too.

**13**

Some things about living in Donner were definitely different. Such as: Mom had stopped reading the newspaper.

For years Mom's paper had been right up there with her love affair with pay phones. It didn't matter where we lived—first thing in the morning and last thing at night, she was hunched over the local paper like a bookie reading *The Racing Form.*

But once we got to Donner, that stopped. Sam had the Coeur d'Alene paper delivered in a metal tube next to the mailbox, but Mom barely glanced at the headlines.

The other thing was: Mom had learned how to cook.

Or maybe she'd known all along, I thought, as I watched her make an omelette one morning, a big puffy one, with cheese and ham and herbs from the garden. Not that I was complaining.

Mary Elizabeth Ryan

Sam wasn't, either. Whatever Mom made, he liked.

"Where'd you learn how to make a pot roast like that, Jenny?" he asked at dinner one night. "I thought you weren't handy in the kitchen."

Mom shrugged. "Maybe I just got tired of having all that money taken out of my pay," she said. "Besides, if you can read a recipe, anyone can cook."

The question was, when did she have time to read cookbooks? As the weather got warmer, business at the nursery had gone into overdrive. All week people had been coming in to buy rosebushes. There must have been some high-frequency rose alert, the way the cars kept pulling up and people rushed in to snap up the roses.

I waited until there was a lull. Then I followed Mom out back.

"I need to go into town. To work on a class assignment."

She paused, her hand wrapped around the thorny trunk of a rosebush.

"Mr. Hatcher—that's our social studies teacher—he's given us this monster project to do on the Vietnam War." I waited while she checked a tag. "We're supposed to talk to people about it. Find out what it was really like."

Major pause.

"Did you ever study that in school, Mom? Like, for current affairs?"

She looked up. "The war? No, I didn't. It wasn't something you talked about in class." She scribbled something on an invoice. "Maybe that's why people protested the war," she went on. "Because no one wanted to talk about it, even the guys who had to go fight it. You didn't talk about it at school, you didn't talk about it at home. It was just this horrible fact of life that you watched on TV every night."

"What did you think about it?" I asked. "Did you ever go on marches and stuff? Or discuss it with your parents?"

I knew she probably wouldn't answer. Mom never talked about her childhood or her parents. But it was worth a shot.

She put down the invoice and gazed at me. "You look thin, kid," she said in a softer tone of voice. "Are you eating the lunches at school? Tell me the truth."

"I'm not thin," I said.

"You have circles under your eyes." She frowned. "Maybe you need to go get a checkup."

"I'm fine. Just a little trouble sleeping."

That was for sure. The dream had come back.

Somehow it had followed me all the way to Idaho and found me. For the past five nights, the train had shown up to take me away. I woke up with its whistle splitting my head.

Mom was picking out a rosebush for a couple waiting out front with Sam. She stood with her back to me, assessing the petals, feeling the leaves.

I knew the rules to this game: When Mom changed the subject, I was dismissed. But I wasn't ready to give up. "How did your brother feel?" I blurted out. "About the war?"

Dumb question, considering he'd died over there. But I wanted to know. Mom had never talked about him, either, except to explain that Fred Hayes was an old friend of Uncle Martin's.

Mom looked up. Her brown eyes were flashing danger. "What on earth are you asking me all this for?"

"We're doing this project—"

"My brother loved this country. He thought he was doing the right thing." The rosebush in her hand began to shake. "He was wrong; he got killed." Mom's eyes suddenly filled with tears. "Please don't ask me to talk about this."

"I'm sorry, Mom. Honest, I just wanted to know . . ."

She picked up the rosebush, thorns and all, and carried it outside.

After a moment, I went outside, too. I waited while Sam wrote up the receipt. "I need a ride into town," I said when he was done. "Mom's too busy to drive me, and I can tell you are, too. Any suggestions?"

"I think the Comptons are heading that way. I'll ask them to give you a lift."

Mom was standing by the car, bundling up the rosebushes. She looked up as Sam walked over to talk to the Comptons.

"Call me when you're done, Toby," she said. "I don't want you walking home on that road."

"Fine. Whatever. Thanks," I told Sam. I helped Mom load the roses and then climbed in the car.

During the ride into town, I sat in back with the rosebushes and talked to Sam's latest customers. Mrs. Compton had grown up around here; Mr. Compton was from Iowa. He moved to Idaho because Iowa was too flat, he said. He worked for a realtor.

"Ever sell any houses to celebrities?" I asked. "My mom told me there were movie stars living around here."

Mr. Compton turned his head around to

laugh. "Movie stars! She must have us confused with Sun Valley. You know, the big ski resort."

"Well, they can have it," Mrs. Compton said emphatically. "Movie stars—no thanks! Next thing you know, we'll have espresso stands and video stores and who knows what all."

Personally, I thought Donner could have used all those things. But I just thanked them when we reached Main Street and crawled out from behind the foliage.

When I reached the Good News Café, Sunny was out front, looking at her watch. She held it up: Disneyland special, Mickey Mouse dressed like a conductor. It was almost two o'clock.

"Hi," she said, "I thought you weren't coming."

"Had to bag a ride," I said. "No more hitch-hiking."

Sunny squinted at me. "I thought you walked."

"Would I tell the sheriff I was hitchhiking?"

She laughed, shrugged, led me inside the café. "You want some tea?"

"Sure."

Sunny disappeared through the bead curtain. I heard her say something in a language that wasn't English. When she came back, she was carrying a pot of tea and two small cups.

"What was that? Cambodian?"

Sunny was cute when she smiled. It didn't happen that often. "Vietnamese," she said.

"No kidding. Can you write it, too?"

"No. I only speak it with my parents. Not even my aunts," she confided. "They don't think I can understand what they're saying, so they talk about me behind my back. 'Naughty girl! American girl!'" Sunny hooted. "Meanwhile, I'm out in the kitchen, listening to every word."

"I thought you were Cambodian."

"Not me—I'm an American. My parents were born in Vietnam. They escaped to Cambodia after 1973."

"You mean after the war?"

"That's what the Vietnamese call it. Things either happened before 1973 or afterwards. My parents don't talk about it much. They stayed in a refugee camp for a long time." Sunny poured me some tea. "Then my aunts came to Canada, and sent for them. My brother and I were born in Seattle."

I tasted my tea while Sunny looked tragic. "Seattle was so cool," she said.

"Why didn't you stay?"

"They didn't like it there. Too many people, drugs, gangs. They were afraid."

"Weren't you?"

"Me? Forget it!"

I had to laugh. "You think you're pretty tough, don't you, Sunny?"

"Hey, and you don't?" Her voice was sharp. "Maybe I don't go around saying my parents came from Vietnam. For sure, not in I-dee-ho."

Sunny sipped her tea. "What are you really doing here?" she asked. Her voice didn't sound angry, just curious. "How come you're living at Sam Wilder's?"

"My mom works there."

"Why did you guys move here?"

I looked around the Good News Café, at the weird posters, the drab furniture, the bead curtain. I pictured Sunny's mom standing behind it, listening.

"Maybe we should talk about our project for Hatcher's class," I said.

Sunny sighed. "You sound just like my parents," she said. "They always change the subject, too."

She opened her notebook. "This is what I came up with," she said. She held out a typed page. "I got a computer for Christmas," she added. "I'm getting pretty good with it."

I looked at the page. It was an essay about Sunny's parents.

"My grammar's not so hot," she said, fidgeting with the notebook.

I ignored her and focused on the essay. It was pretty tough going. She wrote about what her parents went through at the hands of the Khmer Rouge. How most of their family died in Vietnam or Cambodia, except for the aunts who made it to Canada. How they felt ashamed of their English, when people made fun of their accents. How they'd worked to make a life in a country that used to be their enemy.

"It's good," I said. "I tried to talk to my mom about how she felt about the war," I added. "She changed the subject."

"Yeah," said Sunny.

We sipped our cold tea.

"Maybe you could do a research paper," she suggested after a moment. "You know, go online?"

"That's right, you have a computer. Wish I had one."

"My parents got it so I could ace all my classes. But I have to let my brother use it, too." She sighed. "He only plays games on it."

"Can I see it?"

Sunny glanced at the back of the restaurant. "We're closed tomorrow," she said. "My parents are going to Copper City to buy supplies. Why don't you come back then? I'll show you how to surf the Net. It's cool!"

I got up to go. Then I paused. "I hope you're not sorry you got stuck doing this with me, Sunny."

Sunny squinted up at me. "Not really," she said slowly. "At first I thought you were kind of weird. But now I think you're okay. I mean, I feel like I can talk to you."

I nodded. "That's cool," I said, even though I couldn't imagine feeling that way. I'd never felt that way, as long as I could remember.

I went over to the pay phone to call Mom. While I was dialing Sam's number, I glanced back at the booth. Sunny was gone.

Then I heard voices in the kitchen: It was Sunny, the American girl, talking to her mom in Vietnamese.

14

I was sitting on the curb in front of the auto supply store when Mom pulled up in the Shark.

"Hey there," she called. "Hop in."

I got in. "Is the rose attack over?" I asked. "Everything under control?"

Mom reached over and squeezed my hand. Kiss and make up time. "Sorry I gave you a hard time. All those orders got me kind of rattled."

"No sweat," I said.

We breezed through town, took the cutoff, and headed back toward the nursery. "Those Comptons were pretty nice people," I said, to fill up the silence.

"Oh yeah? What did you talk about?"

I put my feet up on the dash, and waited for Mom to knock them back off. When she didn't, I sprawled back against the seat. "Mr. Compton sells houses around here. Hasn't sold one to a movie star, though."

Mom raised her eyebrows. "They can't be very big houses," she remarked.

"You told me that you read about this place in a magazine. How it was home to the stars and all that. Well, guess what, Mom? You were only off by a couple hundred miles!"

Mom stared out the Shark's tinted window. The dense, green, celebrity-free landscape closed in on either side of the car. When Mom spoke, her voice was sharp. "So what's the point?"

"No point. But unless Donner is some secret resort for the rich and famous that nobody knows about, I'm kind of curious what we're doing here."

Her hands held the wheel steady. I saw her swallow, saw the hard, controlled smile settle on her face.

"Maybe I just told you that to make you want to come here. Honestly, you should have seen your face when I said Idaho, Toby. You'd have thought we were moving to Nome, Alaska!"

"Why Idaho, Mom?"

"Why not?" Not quite so controlled this time. "It was time to leave L.A. You said so yourself—"

"Bakersfield's a lot shorter drive."

She hit the brakes so hard, my feet almost went through the windshield. I lowered my shoes to the floor. My knees were trembling.

"Don't you interrogate me, Toby Chase. Who do you think you are?"

"Parker," I said. "It's Parker, remember?"

Mom grabbed me by the shoulder, hard. "What is the matter with you?"

That's when I heard it. We both did: the crunch of tires on the shoulder behind us.

Cop tires.

Mom's mouth clamped shut. A blank look filled her eyes as she peered into the rearview mirror. But it was too late. Footsteps approached the Shark.

A man's shirt filled the window behind her head. Not a tan sheriff's uniform. It was an Idaho state trooper.

Mom unrolled the window. "Yes, Officer?"

Sunglasses on a young face bent down to inspect us. "Having car trouble, ma'am?" the trooper asked. Bland. Polite.

"No, sir."

"Thought maybe you were, when I saw you veer off the road."

"Just having a few words with my son here."

He looked past her at me. I tried to smile, but Mom's nervousness was getting to me. I settled for a blank stare.

"This isn't the best place to park, ma'am. It's a

two-lane road. There's a rest area up by the Forest Road turnoff that'll take you off the lane of travel."

Mom nodded. "Good point. I'll remember that." I saw her hand twitch toward the keys in the ignition.

The trooper must have seen it, too. He straightened but kept his fingers poised lightly on the side of the car. "You an Idaho resident?" he asked.

"No, sir," Mom said. "We're just staying up the road. . . ."

My eyes were fixed on the trooper's fingers. Go with the flow. No matter what she says, go along with it. Don't look surprised. Don't look anything.

"Did you know those California plates are expired?" he said finally.

From where I sat I couldn't see the trooper's face, only his thick leather belt, the gun and radio hanging from his hip.

Mom heaved a big sigh. "Oh, darn," she said. "Really?"

"Mind if I take a look at your license, ma'am?"

Mom didn't miss a beat. "No, of course not," she said. She reached down to get her purse. I saw the trooper take a few steps back. Did he think she was armed?

Alias

"I feel so silly," she said as she drew out her wallet. "When we left San Francisco, I had a list a mile long. Guess I never got to the part about renewing—"

"Please remove the license," he interrupted as she offered him the wallet. I watched her take out the plastic card and hand it out the window.

He studied it, looked at Mom, looked at me, looked back at the driver's license.

"It's a terrible picture!" Mom said.

The young trooper smiled. "Yeah, aren't they all."

Unasked questions, unspoken thoughts zoomed through my brain. I suddenly had to go to the bathroom. I suddenly noticed my left foot was asleep. I suddenly wanted to get out of there more than anything I'd ever wanted in my life.

Just when I thought I was going to explode, his hand reappeared at Mom's shoulder. The trooper was holding out her license.

He leaned forward, and then paused, like a minister about to deliver the Sunday sermon.

"All right, Mrs. Parker," he said. "This is a state road, and I could give you a ticket for that expired tab. But since you're a visitor, I'm going to settle for a warning instead."

"Thank you so much—"

"I'd advise you to take care of that as soon as you return to San Francisco. Otherwise you'll have to take your vehicle off the road."

"I understand, sir. Thank you very, very much."

"Have a nice afternoon." The uniform retreated. A minute later, the trooper's car backed up and pulled smoothly past us.

Mom drooped over the steering wheel and closed her eyes. Her license had dropped onto the seat. I picked it up and looked at it.

Jennifer Parker, it said. 544 Elizabeth Street, San Francisco. I remembered the street. It was Carol's address.

"You're right," I said as Mom reached for the license and stuck it back in her wallet. "Terrible picture."

Follow my lead. Don't ask questions, questions, questions....

She waited until the trooper was halfway to Copper City before she pulled back onto the road. This time my feet stayed planted on the floor of the car.

I thought of all the stuff I could have asked. But I didn't have to. The answers were sitting right there, waiting.

They'd been waiting for years.

Carol had gotten her that license before we even arrived.

Mom's names didn't just pop into her head. Things were already set up, worked out, arranged. The arrangements came with licenses, Social Security numbers, histories. They came with maps of Texas, directions to nurseries, stories to tell dumb old Toby.

And the stories didn't feel good anymore.

Mary Elizabeth Ryan

That night I didn't say much to Mom, even though she kept asking how my schoolwork was going, who was in my group for Hatcher's project—stuff I never thought she'd care about in a million years. I kept remembering the look on her face when that cop pulled up behind us. Whatever was going on, it was really starting to spook me.

Watching her bustle around Sam's kitchen, feed Edgar, help Sam with his bookkeeping, I felt the way I had at Carol's house. Like I was caught inside a movie, only I didn't know my lines and no one had told me the plot.

"I'm turning in," I said, even though it was barely nine o'clock. They both looked up from the ledgers.

"Good-night, Toby. I'll be down soon."

"'Night, Mom. 'Night, Sam."

When I got to the cabin, I flopped on my bed. I didn't feel sleepy, I just wanted to be alone. I pulled out my duffel bag and opened the chess box, as if some clue from the past might jump up and hit me in the face.

As I stared at the box of junk, I thought about the day we'd pulled into Donner, how I kept waiting for the map to tell us where we were.

I was still lost. But the only map I had was the one that ran through my dreams.

Or was it?

A nervous feeling filled my stomach, as an idea formed in my head. I knew what I was going to do. *Had* to do.

I shoved aside the curtain and headed out to the main room, where Mom kept her things.

I tried the bureau first. Rummaging through Mom's clothes, I felt like a burglar. Pretty crazy, considering the risks I'd taken when I was swiping stuff. But this was different.

I glanced around the room, trying to figure where she might have hidden it. My eyes fell on an old sea chest at the foot of the bed. I tried the catch. It opened.

Inside, sheets, blankets, towels. I shoved them aside. A second later my fingers touched something hard. I lifted it out.

The box was old and worn from years of travel. The stars and crescents were faded, the cardboard lid frayed at the edges. My hands were shaking so badly, I almost dropped it.

I paused a moment and listened. Was something ticking inside the box?

Nope—just the alarm clock in the corner. I swallowed a few times, took a deep breath, and opened the box.

Inside lay a pile of faded documents. On top was a birth certificate in the name of Jennifer Parker. Underneath were more birth certificates. I recognized Nancy Johnson, Annette Farrell, and some more names Mom had used in the places we'd lived. Others didn't look familiar at all.

I scooped out the contents and found a stack of IDs: driver's licenses and Social Security cards matching the names on the birth certificates. A few library cards, even some voter registration forms.

Some names and telephone numbers were scribbled on a piece of notebook paper. A couple looked familiar. The Miller family in South Dakota, where we spent Christmas one year. A guy in Boston. Carol.

Scattered among the papers were odds and ends, bits and pieces. I picked up a tiny scrap of cloth: a baby's sock. Was it once mine? A ring and a bracelet, tickets to a Chicago Cubs game from

1970, a handkerchief, a button that said in purple letters, Celebrate Poetry.

At the bottom of the box were some pictures. One showed a smiling, bearded man balancing a little kid on his lap. The man was sitting on a lawn chair in an overgrown garden, holding the baby's wrists with his hands.

My heart began hammering like a locomotive. I huddled closer to the lamp, straining my eyes for details of the man's face, but the picture was too old and faded—all I could make out were the beard and the smile.

And the ears.

I was reaching for the other pictures when the door to the cabin slammed shut. I looked up to see Mom standing over me.

"What are you doing?" she asked, even though it was pretty obvious.

Before I could say anything, she walked over and took the empty box out of my hands. The contents were still strewn all over the bed. I watched Mom scoop everything up and put it back in the box.

When she was done, she turned and glared at me. "You'd better have a damn good reason for this, Toby."

"I do," I said. "I'd kind of like to know what's going on—"

"What's going on is that I come in here and find you going through my things." She shook her head. "I've always respected your privacy. I'm really disappointed you can't respect mine."

A thought sprang into my head: She was stalling.

"What's the deal with all the fake paper?" I said. "Birth certificates, IDs . . . Are you an illegal alien, Mom? Visitor from another planet?"

Mom shook her head. "You've seen too many movies, Junior." I watched her lift the lid to the chest and tuck the box back under the blankets.

"This isn't some game," I said, "right, Mom? I used to think you just made it up. The names, the moves, everything. But today, in the car...."

Mom turned around. "Is that what this is about, Toby? That stupid business with the license plates? Look, it was just a dumb mistake. . . ."

"What about the license with Carol's address? Those birth certificates?"

Mom sighed. "It's called starting over, Toby. Lots of people do it. People with bad credit, people who make mistakes. Trust me, it's not that uncommon."

I blinked at her. "You don't have bad credit, Mom," I said. "How could you? You always pay for everything in cash."

She began straightening the bed. When she'd finished, she turned to face me.

"Listen to me, Toby. Sometimes things happen in a person's life that they can't control. The road isn't always straight and the path isn't always narrow."

I didn't know what she was talking about, but I nodded.

"When I was a lot younger, I got into some trouble. Some of it was just bad judgment. The point is that I'm not afraid to start over. To be somebody else for a while, if I have to."

I swallowed. "What did you do, Mom? Did you take something that didn't belong to you?"

She shook her head. "It's nothing like that. And nothing for you to worry about. Because we're here now, and things are fine. Better than they've been in a long time. So please, relax."

I stood there, wondering why I couldn't relax, why I couldn't accept what she was saying.

"That guy in the picture," I said finally. "Was that my dad?"

Mom was silent for a moment. I saw her glance down at the chest, as if she were looking at the picture herself.

"No," she said.

She came over to where I was standing and

put her arms around me. "That man in the picture holding the baby? That's your grandpa. And that funny-looking little kid he's holding? That was me."

I felt her arms tighten around me. I didn't know what to say, what to think.

"He's got my ears," I said finally.

When I went up to the house the next morning, I was surprised to see Sam wearing a jacket and tie.

"Morning," he said. "Thought I'd take your mom to the Palm Sunday service. She's sold flowers to half the congregation this week. Figured I'd give 'em a chance to see her without the dirt under her fingernails." He smoothed his tie. "You're welcome to come along, Toby."

I grabbed some coffee. "Thanks," I said, "but I've got some stuff to do in town."

"Stuff involving a girl, maybe?"

The fatherly way he said it made me pause. "It's for school," I said. "Maybe you guys could drop me off."

Sam watched me drink my coffee. "Church is in the other direction," he said. He scratched his head. "Looks like you could use some transportation of your own."

"Looks that way," I said. "But no way Mom will let me drive the car."

"Got an idea." With a mysterious grin, he stepped outside.

I put down my coffee and followed him to the garage. A second later he came out, wheeling a ten-speed bike.

"That's for me?"

"It was my son's," he said. "I polished up the frame. Put some air in the tires. And—" he tossed me a white bike helmet. "This should keep your brain in one piece."

"Assuming it still is."

One, two, three . . .

Sam smiled. "Its original condition, then."

I studied the bike. I hadn't been on one in a while. Not since I graduated to skateboarding.

"Hey, thanks," I said. "Sure beats scrounging rides."

He looked pleased. Sam Wilder was not hard to read.

I climbed on the bike. While I was pedaling around the yard, Mom came up the path. She was wearing a new blue dress. She had a lace shawl around her shoulders. She looked extremely pretty.

She laughed when she saw me on the bike.

"You'll never see that boy again," she said to Sam.

Whatever Sam felt when he looked at Mom wasn't hard to read, either. I pointed the bike at the path and took my feet off the pedals. In a minute I was plunging down the incline, coasting to a stop in front of the Shark.

"Be careful, Toby!" Mom called after me. But by then I could hardly hear her.

Sunny was all business when I got to the Good News Café. As soon as I rode up, she led me to her family's apartment behind the restaurant.

"My parents will be back in a couple hours," she said. "Stephen, my little brother, went with them. Once he gets home, it'll be impossible to do anything."

We went in Sunny's room. Very Sunny—fashion pictures on the walls, boring-looking computer manuals piled next to the bed.

"You're pretty into this stuff," I said as she sat down at the computer.

She looked up. "Aren't you?"

"Computers are okay. But I can't picture sitting up all night reading about them."

She grabbed the mouse. "Hey, good luck," she said. "Sounds like you have a swell future lined up in the fast-food industry."

That shut me up. I sat down next to the computer and watched Sunny do her stuff.

"What are we looking for?" she asked.

I thought about it. I didn't know. Then I remembered the story Sheriff Springer had told about his brother. "Try antiwar protests," I said.

Images from the sixties flooded the screen. Mass marches and teach-ins, people holding signs, shouting slogans, a guy sticking a flower into the barrel of a gun.

We checked out the riots during the Democratic Convention in 1968, how the police charged into groups of longhaired kids, wielding batons and tear gas, cracking skulls, dragging people away by their hair. And the Kent State massacre in 1970, when the National Guard opened fire on a protest rally in Ohio, killing four students. We listened to folk singers and rock groups, ministers and news reporters, Black Panthers and Yippies, until I began to feel dizzy.

"Can you check out some newspapers?" I asked. "Hatcher said he wanted this to be real. Maybe I can get some quotes. You know, eyewitness stuff."

Sunny typed in more commands. My eyes blurred as pages of print flooded the screen.

We looked at stories about the marches, the

Chicago convention. The SDS, the Weathermen, Kent State. More sidebars, more newspapers, more everything.

"Make up your mind," Sunny said. She pushed her chair back and stretched. "I'm getting hungry."

I glanced at the screen, wondering what to do.

Then I saw something that made me stop wondering.

It was a small blurry picture in the left-hand corner of the article. It showed a young, dark-haired woman with her head thrown back.

"Fugitives Sought in Antiwar Conspiracy," the headline read. It was from the *Chicago Sun-Times,* May 15, 1970. The group was called Students for Peace; police had raided their headquarters on an anonymous tip and found incendiary devices, enough explosives to blow up a building. Their target was the university ROTC recruiting center. Most of the Students for Peace had been arrested, the article said, but three members of the group were still sought for questioning.

Their names were listed under each fuzzy photograph: "Ron Kantor, 22; Barbara Gordon, 20; Anne Freeman, 19."

I studied the dark-haired girl again. Off in the

distance I could hear the mournful blast from the Burlington Northern as it rumbled by on its way to Canada, but it could have been the train from my dream.

Anne Freeman was my mother.

It was like an accident. You see the car a second before it hits you. Part of you knows what's happening, but some other part doesn't want to believe, won't believe. Until the crash comes.

I sat in Sunny Thieu's bedroom and watched the pieces of my weird life fall into place. It wasn't the pattern I expected. But at least it made sense:

*Click.* We moved around because Mom was a fugitive. She used different aliases so no one would find out who she really was.

*Click.* If it's Boston, Mom must be Nancy. Don't ask questions. Don't talk to anyone. Keep your mouth shut. Even if they tell you she's dead.

*Click.* No phone, in case anyone checked telephone records. No Visa cards—you'd need a credit history for that, even a bad one. No bank account; after all, they nabbed Al Capone for tax evasion. Then again, you can't owe taxes if you don't exist.

I glanced at Sunny. She wasn't even looking at the computer. She was staring at the door.

"I just heard my parents' car pull up," she said. "They must have gotten back early."

"No problem," I said. "I think I've seen enough."

Sunny started to exit the database.

"Wait," I said. "Can you print out that last file? There's some stuff in there I want to use in my report."

"What stuff?" Sunny stared at me impatiently.

"Just some stuff from that article. I thought it had some good quotes."

Sunny shrugged. She hit the mouse, and a page slid out of the printer. I folded it and shoved it in my pack. I was reaching for my bike helmet when Sunny's little brother slammed into the room.

"You guys done yet?" he said, wedging himself in front of the computer. He hit a key, and the picture of Mom abruptly vanished.

"Stephen!" Sunny rolled her eyes. She got up and walked me out to the restaurant where her parents were unloading boxes. They glanced up and smiled at me, but I ducked my head.

I was never here. Annie Chase/Jenny Parker/Anne Freeman doesn't exist. Neither does her kid.

The sun was still shining when I climbed on my new bike, but I didn't notice.

Mom, I know who you are.

If I could find you, they can find us.

We've been pulled over on the Information Superhighway, and this time they won't let us off with a warning.

I began to pedal down the street. When I reached the corner, one of the straps from my pack slid down my shoulder. While I was fixing it, a big Greyhound bus came lumbering up the street on its weekly run from Coeur d'Alene to British Columbia.

I watched it wheeze to a stop in front of the general store that doubled as the local bus depot. A few people got off and stood blinking in the sun while the driver reached into the luggage bay to pull out their suitcases.

I was about to take off when one of the passengers caught my attention. He was a tall guy dressed in tan pants and a leather jacket. He stood in the shadow of the awning, chatting with a couple of women who were waiting for their luggage. Even with his back to me, there was something familiar about him.

As I watched from the corner, the man reached in his pocket and pulled out a pack of smokes. He turned out of the wind, struggling to light up.

*Click.* The thin build, the silver hair, the cigarette dangling from his mouth. Even without the shoe polish beard, I knew why he seemed so familiar, and the knowledge sent my heart thudding to my toes.

It was Bad News Fred.

Heading south, the road was straight downhill; I practically coasted all the way to Sam's.

I wheeled the bike into the garage, and then stood there in the dark, trying to sort out my thoughts. What was Fred Hayes doing in Donner? How did he know we were here? Had Mom written him from the nursery? Had he seen me?

I wasn't sure. But I knew one thing. When Bad News Fred showed up, it was time to move on.

And I knew something else. He knows who Mom is, I thought. He's always known.

I went up the slope to the backyard with its row of apple trees. I raised my arms and rested my weight against the crooked branches. I saw Sam come out of the nursery and whistle for Edgar, and they headed up toward the house. He'd changed out of his church clothes, I noticed. I pictured Mom sitting through the service next to Sam, the whole church full of people staring at them, mur-

muring about it over their Sunday dinners.

I peered down the hill. An ancient taxi was moving slowly along the main road. It pulled in at the gate and wound around the curve, heading for the nursery.

He'd brought luggage: a backpack and brief-case. They lay at his feet in the parking lot while old Fred paid the fare, hitched up his belt, and took a look around.

I saw him glance up at the house and then back at the nursery. After a couple of moments he picked up his things and walked toward the green-house.

Sam was in the kitchen. He glanced up when I came in. "I thought we'd have ham for dinner—"

"Someone's here," I reported. "A friend of Mom's. Fred Hayes."

Sam stared at me. After a moment he nodded. "Fine," he said. "Aren't you going to bring him inside?"

I heard footsteps on the porch. Then the door opened, and Fred appeared.

He paused in the doorway. "Is this the right place?" he called, then smiled when he saw me. "Toby! Let's take a look at you, buddy. You're all grown up!"

"How you doing," I offered.

Fred was really making an effort. Sam stood behind me, watching.

"Fred Hayes," I said, "this is Sam Wilder, Mom's boss. He owns this place."

"Glad to meet you," Sam said. He reached for Fred's hand just as Mom came in, carrying Fred's bags.

"Oh, good," she said, putting down the brief-case and pack. "You've met."

I could read the surprise and confusion on Sam's face. Fred Hayes was definitely not what Sam had in mind for Palm Sunday.

"Fred's an old friend," Mom told Sam. "From years ago."

"I was just passing through," Fred explained, "and I remembered a postcard I'd gotten from Jenny here. Thought I'd take a chance and look her up."

Sam sat down at the table. "How long will you be staying, Mr. Hayes? It's a little early for the tourist season."

"Actually, I'm traveling on business. I'm afraid I can only spend a few hours. Duty calls."

"What business did you say you were in, Mr. Hayes?"

"Corporate relocation," Fred told him. "We move executives and their families when they're transferred around the country. And—it's Fred."

I thought of all the times Mom and I had moved. All the cities, the states, the different schools. Corporate relocation? More like pieces on a chessboard, I thought. And Fred was the grand master.

"Wish I could have given Jen more warning," Bad News Fred was saying, "but like I said—just took a chance I'd catch her."

He turned to Mom. "Did you say there was a motel nearby, Jenny? I'm just dead on my feet."

"There's a bed-and-breakfast near the free-way," Sam said. "If you drove up from Boise you must have seen it."

"Guess I missed it. I took a cab from town."

I watched Sam ponder that. I pondered it, too. But now I understood: Buses and cabs were safer. No credit card receipts, no gas records, no license plates. Fred knew the value of cash. Just like Mom.

"Maybe you could join us for Sunday dinner, Mr. Hayes," Sam said. "Give you and Jenny a chance to catch up. In the meantime, why don't I give you the tour and let you wash up." He led Fred through the living room. I heard their voices retreat as they went up the stairs.

I turned to Mom. "Some surprise, huh?"

The smile that had been on her face the whole

time was gone. "Yes, a surprise," she said. "Good old Fred."

Throughout the meal, Fred did most of the talking. I listened to him drone on about the great scenery, what a fabulous place Sam had. While he was talking, I slipped Edgar most of my ham.

Afterward Sam went out to check on the nursery, and Fred went with him. My hands moved mechanically through the soapy water. Mom dried each dish as I passed it to her. There were a million things I wanted to say, but I felt like there was a brick stuck in my throat.

When Sam came back, he was alone.

"Where's Fred?" Mom asked as she dried the last fork.

"Out on the porch, smoking," Sam said.

He started toward his office. At the door he stopped. "Jenny, this is none of my business. But is there something I should know about this guy?"

Mom's face reddened. "Fred? He's just an old friend. But I'll speak to him about the cigarettes, if you like."

"It's not that," Sam said. He hesitated.

"Everything's fine, Sam. But thanks for the concern." Mom's voice was abrupt, impatient.

I felt sorry for Sam. He didn't know he'd broken the rule about asking Mom questions. He just looked zapped.

Sam cleared his throat. "Well, I'm here if you need anything." He turned and went into the living room. We heard the swivel chair squeak as he sat down at his desk.

Mom put down the fork she was holding. She gestured toward the door. Silently I followed her outside.

Fred stood on the porch, puffing on a cigarette, shoulders hunched in his suede jacket.

Staring at Fred's skinny form, I suddenly realized he knew more about my life than I did, that it gave him power over me. Over both of us. It didn't make me like him any better.

He smiled when he saw us. "Beautiful out here," he called.

"Yes, it is," Mom answered. She paused to admire the view—the nursery nestled in the hollow, the snowcapped mountains beyond.

"I should be taking off soon," he said.

"I'll give you a ride when you're ready."

"Thanks," Fred said. He laughed. "Believe me, one trip in Ed's Taxi Express was plenty."

"I'll go get my coat," Mom said. She started down the steps.

I nodded at Fred. "Hey, Fred, take it easy."

"You too, Toby. You keep eating those Idaho spuds. They agree with you."

"Will do."

I waited until we got inside. I watched Mom reach for her jacket, check for her keys.

"The Shark's okay?" I asked.

She nodded. "Sam took care of it on Monday. Everything's nice and legal now. No more heart attacks."

"We're leaving, aren't we," I said.

She paused. "Now why on earth would you think that?"

"I don't know. Just a hunch."

Mom pulled on her jacket. She was still wearing the nice dress from church. She looked slightly out of breath.

"Well, you guessed wrong," she said. She tossed the car keys in her pocket, and left.

I gave her a head start. Moving like a cat, I slipped outside and took the path that ran behind the greenhouse.

I edged behind the building, and squeezed between the shrubbery and the wall. Then I pressed my ear against the cold glass. Voices bounced against the window.

"We were worried when we didn't hear anything," Fred was saying.

"Well, you shouldn't have been. Toby and I are doing fine up here. You see how it is. Isn't this place great?"

"Anne . . ."

There was a long pause. When Mom finally spoke, her voice was low, intense.

"If you're asking why I haven't answered the ads, the answer's simple, Fred. I didn't want to. And please put that cigarette out. The plants don't like smoke."

"You didn't want to? What in hell were you thinking?" Fred's thin voice cracked with exasperation. "Do you know how *stupid* that is?" I heard him sigh. "Annie, where is your brain? What's happened to you?"

"Nothing, Fred. And it's Jenny, remember?" She walked farther up the rows, and I moved with her.

Fred followed her, too. This time I didn't need to press my ear to the window; his voice was loud with anger. "Two months with no word! Peter was ready to write you off, but I convinced him to let me come up here instead."

"What's the big deal? The Network knows where I am."

"That's not the point," Fred said, and he sounded genuinely pissed. "You know the drill.

After you left San Francisco, you were supposed to make your calls, answer the ads, keep the Network posted, set up your backup plan."

He sounded like Hatcher ragging on us to get our assignments in on time.

"You haven't done any of that stuff," Fred said. "You're getting sloppy, Anne."

"No, Fred," Mom said, "I'm just getting tired."

Silence.

"Look," he said finally, "you wanted to get out of the city, we got you out of the city. Small towns are riskier, but hey, you were worried about your kid."

"Yes, I was. Thank you, Fred."

"You should have stayed closer to town. I had a hell of a time even finding this place."

"Isn't that the point?"

"The point is, if anything went wrong—"

"But it won't, Fred. Tell Peter we want to stay awhile."

More silence. "Awhile isn't forever."

"Didn't say it was, Fred." Mom bent down to pick up Fred's bags. "Now," she said, "how about that ride?"

The glass was getting pretty fogged up. I rubbed a space with my palm. I saw Fred's thin form pause at the door.

"There's something else. Something I have to tell you."

I couldn't see what he was doing—taking something out of his pocket, I guessed. He handed whatever it was to Mom.

Immediately I heard a low noise. It sounded like Edgar, the way he groaned in his sleep. With a sick feeling, I realized it was coming from Mom.

"I wasn't supposed to show you this. But it didn't seem right. Better you heard it from me. That way—"

He didn't finish. The awful sound grew louder as Mom began to cry.

# 17

I dreamed I was in a jungle. Thick growth, dark shadows. The jungle smelled of rotting petunias and fertilizer, like a big greenhouse.

Vines slapped my face as I made my way along the jungle floor. I dreamed that a silent lion was following my every step. I'd go one way, sure I was safe, only to find the lion already there, waiting for me.

"What are you doing in the jungle?" I asked the lion. "You live on the African plain. I learned that somewhere, at one of my schools."

The lion said nothing. Its eyes were depthless with understanding. I noticed, right before it sprang, that it didn't have a mane. It was a female.

I woke up, confused and restless. I rolled over and peered at the clock: six A.M. Finally I got up and pulled back the curtain.

Mom's bed was empty.

My heart hammered like crazy. I scrambled into my clothes and hurled myself outside. Cold air filled my lungs. Frost crunched under my feet as I ran up the path to Sam's house. No lights were on. I stopped when I reached the porch.

A dozen thoughts hit me, all of them bad. She must have left with Fred. Whatever it was he'd shown her, it was enough to make her leave. Or she just wanted to take off. Maybe she was fed up with dragging me along.

Or maybe she was inside with Sam....

"Toby?"

Mom stood below me on the path. She was wearing a nightgown and boots, a windbreaker thrown over her shoulders.

"I heard the dog barking," she said. "I thought maybe the deer were getting into the seedlings again."

Then she gave me a puzzled smile. "What are you doing out," she asked, "without your shoes?"

I looked down and saw I was barefoot.

"You were gone when I woke up," I said. I felt like I was whining, but I didn't care. "I thought you'd—"

"Gone? Well, I couldn't get too far without my navigator. Could I?"

I suddenly felt stupid. Mom wouldn't leave without the box, without the Once-Over. Without even saying good-bye.

The ground was cold under my feet. I began to hop up and down. Mom pulled her windbreaker around her. "Look at us, Tobe. Like a couple of sleepwalkers out here."

I nodded. "Yeah, pretty weird."

"Come on," she said. "Race you back."

I followed Mom down the path, watching the long nightgown brush the tops of her boots. I felt like Fred Hayes: Now I was the one with the secret, the power. But instead of making me feel powerful, it scared me.

Back in the chilly cabin, Mom jabbed kindling in the Franklin stove to make a fire. After a few tries, it began to burn, snapping loudly as the sap spat into the flames.

Mom came over to the table. "Challenge you to a game of double solitaire," she said. She cleared off the center of the table. "I'll make some tea. You run and get the cards."

"I don't think we brought any, Mom."

"Well, I know we have checkers. Get the board—scoot."

I pictured the board, folded up in my duffel bag. "I'm not really in the mood," I said.

"Come on, Toby. It'll be fun. Just the two of us. I've missed that."

I thought about it. "Yeah, me, too."

I went and got the checker set. "Okay," I said. "Prepare to meet your doom."

I unfolded the red-and-black board on the table. When I opened it, something fell out. Mom picked it up.

It was her picture.

"What's this?" she said. Her eyes were flashing. "Where on earth did you get this, Toby?"

I couldn't lie anymore. I was sick of telling lies, sick of hearing them. "At Carol's house," I said.

Mom's face looked like one of those time-lapse photographs, a dozen different emotions sliding across it, one after another. A dozen different people.

She stared at the picture. "I haven't seen this in years," she said. "I didn't know Carol had it."

"You weren't at college together, Mom."

She glanced up. "What are you talking about?"

"You didn't know Carol at college. She said you went to high school together, but I don't think that's true, either." I took a deep breath. "You went to school in Chicago. That's where the trouble happened. Didn't it, Mom?"

Silence. She didn't move, but I saw her jaw tighten.

"But here's the crazy part," I said. "Even at Carol's, I still didn't get it. You showed up on my friend's computer. On the Internet." I swallowed. "I wish you'd told me. Why didn't you, Mom?"

Mom was staring down at the picture. Her face wore only one emotion now: very sad.

"I wanted to be an actress," she said after a moment. "Kind of funny, isn't it? I went to Chicago because of their drama school. My parents wanted me to stay near home. I just wanted to get away. . . ."

She sighed and touched the face of the laughing girl. "When I was nineteen," she said, "the Vietnam War was at its height. We thought it was going to last forever. Boys dying for nothing, and nobody would do anything to stop it. When my brother was killed, I joined a student protest group."

"Where was this?" I asked.

"Chicago University. I remember painting my face white and marching into the faculty senate, chanting, 'End the War.' We called it guerrilla theater. It sounds silly now, but we were very serious. Everyone was."

"The Students for Peace?"

"That's what we called ourselves. It wasn't a bunch of wild-eyed radicals, mostly just scared kids." Mom sighed. "The bombing in Cambodia began, and then the shootings at Kent State. We felt so helpless. Until someone in the group came up with a plan: getting the explosives, a map of the building, finding out when the office would be empty."

Her eyes were glued to the table. My eyes were glued to her face.

"The night before it was supposed to happen, someone tipped off the authorities. We were meeting in an apartment, near school. All of a sudden these agents burst through the door, flashing their badges, arresting people. Somehow I got out. I hid in a basement. Someone brought me food. After three days a guy showed up and drove me to another city. I never went back to college. I never told my parents, back in Philadelphia. I never became an actress. I went underground."

Mom cleared her throat. "The people who rescued me were part of an organization for political fugitives. There were a lot of us back then. Not so many now . . . most of the people I knew were arrested, charged with conspiracy, sentenced. I was luckier. I met Peter."

"Peter?"

"I don't know much about him. But he has a lot of connections—the Network. The idea is to keep moving around, but still staying in touch with the Network. Peter. Or the people he assigns, like Carol and Fred."

"What's the deal with Fred?" I asked.

Mom paused. "Fred is my contact, has been for years. Mostly it's done through ads in the newspaper or post office boxes. If Fred thinks things are heating up, he places an ad. Something like 'Found: diamond wristwatch, initial F on the band; call this number.' That's how I know to contact him for instructions."

My head began to hurt. I wished this dream would end, that I'd wake up to the familiar sound of gunshots on Dolores Street, to my terrifying but predictable life at Fillmore High.

"What about those birth certificates?" I asked.

"It's not difficult to find a deceased person the right age." She shrugged. "The Network arranged everything."

Silence.

"So who's Annie Chase?" I asked then.

"Chase? That was your grandmother's maiden name."

"Your mom's, you mean?"

"Jack's."

Major silence.

"Did Dad know about . . . all this stuff?" I asked. "Who you were and everything?"

"Of course!" She stared at me, indignant. "It was the only thing I could do. We met in Hawaii, got married, moved to Colorado. That's where you were born. When it was time to leave, Jack wanted to come, too. He would have, except someone driving home from a bar prevented him."

Mom traced a finger across the squares on the board.

"There's something else, Toby." Her face was weirdly calm, like those people they lead out of burning buildings on the news.

"What?"

"My mother's dead. She had cancer for a long time. Fred showed me the obituary last night." Mom paused. "I can't even go to her funeral. My own mother."

Her shoulders began to shake, but she didn't make a sound.

"Why don't you turn yourself in?" I said it very quickly; anyone with two brain cells to rub together would already know the answer, but I made myself ask anyway.

The shaking stopped. When Mom looked up, her eyes shone like steel.

"Because," she said, "I'd go to jail, Toby." Her voice was so matter-of-fact, it chilled me. She sounded like Sam explaining how to repot a begonia without damaging the roots. "My name's on lists, unsolved crime files. All I have is the

Network to keep me safe. To keep us invisible."

"But you're not invisible," I told her. "I was researching this paper for school, and there you were, in some database...."

Mom smiled faintly. "I'm in a lot of them, I'm sure."

"Aren't you scared?"

"No one in this little town is going to connect me to something that happened in Chicago twenty years ago."

That's when I heard it: a knock at the door. My heart slammed against the walls of my chest. For a moment Mom and I just looked at each other.

Then she got up, blew her nose, pulled her jacket around her nightgown, and went to answer the door.

Sam stood in the door. I couldn't tell whether he'd heard anything; I doubted it. Sam wasn't the type who would eavesdrop; that was my department.

"Just thought I'd make sure everything's okay," he said as if it was something he did every morning. I saw him peer past her into the cabin. Was he looking for Fred?

"A-OK." Mom gave him a smile. My head still hurt from what she'd just told me, but I noticed that her smile was real.

Sam nodded, slow and thoughtful.

"Hal's up at the house," he said. "Stopped by for breakfast. And to gossip."

I was still at the table, the pile of checkers in front of me. Sam glanced at me. "Says he's got something he wants to ask you, Toby."

My mouth opened, but nothing came out. I gaped at Sam like a beached trout.

"Tell Hal Toby will be right up," Mom said.

Sam nodded again. I got the feeling he would have loved it if Mom invited him in, fixed him a cup of tea, and told him to put his feet up, but she didn't. He paused a second, then bobbed his head and left.

I waited until Mom shut the door. Then I asked, "Is Sam part of this? I mean, he's not like Carol or Fred, part of the Network. Is he?"

Mom smiled. She looked calm now, even relaxed. Her self-control amazed me. "Sam? Sam Wilder? Are you nuts?"

"But if the Network sent you here...."

"They try to help people, Toby, that's all. They can't arrange everything," she said. "I had a list of places to look for work. Sam's Nursery wasn't on it."

"I guess the Network didn't know what it was missing," I said.

Mom sighed. "They sure wouldn't have sent me here if they knew Sam and Hal Springer were old friends," she answered. "Why does the sheriff want to talk to you, Toby?"

I pictured the binoculars sitting in my duffel bag. "Beats me," I said.

"Well, don't keep him waiting." Mom reached for a stack of towels and headed for the shower.

At the bathroom door she paused. "No matter what he asks you, just go with the flow. Stick to the truth as much as possible. It's easier that way."

I stared at her. "What is, Mom?"

"The acting part," she said. "The part where you have to remember what you've said. The trick is to believe every word while you're saying it."

Mom hugged the towels to her chest. "You know, when you go underground, one thing they tell you is never have kids."

"Why's that?"

"Because they're too darn honest," she said.


Sheriff Springer was scratching Edgar behind the ears when I reached the house. I searched his face for some clue, but he just greeted me jovially and went back to talking to Sam about a game poacher he'd bagged on the Connor ranch.

I stood by the stove and got some coffee. Hal glanced at me once or twice; he made a joke about kids who stunt their growth with coffee, but that was all.

Finally he got to his feet.

"Won't keep you from your toils, Mr. Wilder," he said to Sam. "I know you've got a busy one coming up, with Easter next week and all."

"That's a fact," Sam said. "Good to see you,

Hal. Want me to have Toby pick you out a nice Easter lily?"

"No need. I'll bring Maggie by and let her pick one out." He reached down to pat Edgar's broad head. "Toby, why don't you walk me down to the van if you can tear yourself away from that java."

It took me a second to figure out he meant the coffee. Nervously I set it down and followed him.

Sheriff Springer's big feet crunched down the path. When we reached the parking strip, he stopped. Now that we were away from the house, he wasn't smiling.

I tried to give him my best blank stare.

"Toby, I'll be blunt. Bill Saunders told me he asked you to try out for his team, and you turned him down flat." The sheriff's broad forehead wrinkled with annoyance.

Basketball? He was giving me this heart attack over the stupid Rebels?

"Not exactly," I said.

Sheriff Springer shook his head. "'Says he has to work after school.' Those were his exact words. Son, I checked with Sam, and I know you're not exactly on the payroll."

I caught the twinkle in the sheriff's eye. He was playing with me, pulling out his little detective act, enjoying the fact that he was making me sweat.

Mary Elizabeth Ryan

"I didn't realize it was a big deal," I said. "To be honest, I'm not that hot at sports. I don't think the Rebels are missing out on much."

The sheriff hooted. "All those schools back in Texas and California and everywhere—you never passed and dribbled? With those mile-long legs of yours?"

"That's what I'm saying."

Sheriff Springer was starting to get on my nerves. I just wanted him to get in his van and drive away. Instead, he walked over to the Shark.

"Looks like your ma finally got some new plates for this hot rod," he said. He paused to admire the Idaho emblem on the shiny license plate. "Heard she had a little problem up the road with Trooper Myers," he added. "He's pretty hard on the tourists, Carl is."

I gazed levelly back. But I was beginning to wonder what he was up to.

He was kicking idly at the Shark's tires, studying its dented fender, the cracked rear window.

"But then, you're not tourists, are you? You and your mom, you show up here one day, out of the blue. Don't know a soul in town. I can understand how he might make that mistake."

I didn't say a word.

"Well, it's none of my business." Sheriff

Springer grinned. "Your mother seems like a fine person. Sam's taken a real shine to her. I can understand that, too."

The sheriff leaned against the rusting hood of the Shark. "Couple years ago, Sam's wife and son were killed. Terrible tragedy. Logging truck lost its brakes coming over the pass. They didn't stand a chance." The sheriff heaved a sigh. "Laid Sam so low, I wasn't sure he'd ever come out of it. But lately I've seen a big difference. Guess I should be happy for him, right?"

I wished he'd get off our car. Turn around, take his snoopy comments, and leave. But all I could do was listen and go with the flow. Just like Mom said.

Finally the sheriff hitched up his belt and walked over to me. "Sam Wilder trusts people. I don't. Guess it's an occupational hazard." His eyes flickered across my face like he was trying to solve a puzzle.

Then they moved on. I turned to see what he was looking at. Together we watched Mom come out of the cabin dressed in her work clothes.

She caught sight of us and waved. The sheriff raised his arm and waved back. The big smile was back on his face.

"Well, busy day ahead," he said at last, and

Mary Elizabeth Ryan

started for the van. "Remember what I said, Toby. The Rebels need a good starter. Kids they got this year haven't done squat." He pointed at the garage. "You ask Sam to nail a hoop up there for you," he suggested. "Spend the summer practicing. Might be just the ticket."

Sheriff Springer laughed. "Hey, don't mind me, Toby. I talk too much, I guess. You have yourself a great day."

As he was backing out, he suddenly braked and rolled down the window.

"Wouldn't you know it? Nearly forgot why I came out here in the first place."

"What's that?"

"Will you ask Sam if he's seen my Bushnells? Ever since that trip to the lake, they just up and disappeared on me."

"Your Bushnells?"

Sheriff Springer waved a dismissive hand at me. "Just give Sam the message," he called. "He'll know what they are." He gave the horn a blast and spun the wheel. The van rolled down the dirt road.

I went over to the Shark and collapsed against it. My knees were shaking. Everything was shaking.

Finally I hauled myself up and went into the greenhouse. Mom was already in the back, working on some Easter arrangements.

She paused when she saw me. "What do you think? You figure these will sell?"

Her smile faded as she focused on my face. "What is it, Toby? What's wrong?"

I picked up a lily from the basket and folded my hands around it. It was perfect, waxy and white—so perfect, it looked fake.

"He talked to that trooper, Mom," I said. "The one who stopped you."

Mom frowned. "He did?"

"I guess they're friends or something. The guy said we were tourists. I mean, that's what you told him, right?"

Mom took the lily out of my hands and placed it back in the cutting basket. "Plenty of people say they're just passing through," she said, "to cover an expired tab." She was nodding, the wheels turning in her head. "It probably happens every day. Nothing to worry about."

"Yeah. I guess." I watched her pick up a handful of daffodils and set to work.

"So he didn't say anything else?"

"Just bugged me about basketball," I told her. "Wants Sam to put up a hoop so I can sharpen my three-pointers. So I can finally give the Rebels their winning season."

"Is that really all he said, Toby?"

"Honest, Mom. I wouldn't kid you—"

Whoosh! A sack of peat moss came whistling past me.

"Heads up!" Sam stood in the door. "Toby? You want to help me unload some of these?"

"Huh? Oh, yeah." I took the sack and carried it out to the supply shed.

When I came back, Mom was standing outside, next to the truck. She was smiling.

"Did you hear? We're going to the farmers market in Bonners Ferry next week. Just to look around, Sam says. But you never know. Maybe it's time this guy set up a stall of his own."

Mom kept up the chatter about Sam's prospects. How it was time he did more than just grow Christmas trees and sell houseplants to the locals, how he should put his name on the map, a guy with his talent. She was really laying it on with a trowel.

"Hey, let's not get carried away," Sam said, but his eyes were dancing. He was eating it up.

She was still giving him the Annie Chase whammy, I thought. Still working him, like the guy from Tired Tires and Johnny the florist.

Just in case.

I went with the flow. But the bad dreams didn't go away.

At night I wandered through dark jungles, waiting for the lion to pounce, for the train to crash. In class I listened to Hatcher talk about the war, and wondered what he'd think about the nice lady down at Sam's Nursery who sold houseplants. When I was alone, I stared at the story from the *Chicago Sun-Times* from May, 1970, and tried to think what I could put in a social studies report that anyone would believe.

Friday lunchtime. Standing in the post office to buy stamps for Sam, I caught myself staring at the wanted posters hanging on a hook next to the stamp machine.

Cruel faces gazed impassively back: Wanted for armed robbery; Wanted for kidnapping. I was pretty sure Mom's picture wasn't on that peg, but I decided not to check.

That night Mom cooked steaks. Sam made a big deal about how good they tasted, rolling his eyes and sighing until Mom started laughing. Usually I'll eat steak whenever I can get it, but I barely touched mine.

"You feeling okay?" Sam said when I put down my fork and asked to be excused.

"Got a lot of work to do for school," I said. "Think I'll go hit the books, if that's all right. I'll come up later and get those dishes."

Mom glanced up from her steak. "No, you do your homework, Toby. I'll take care of things."

I went and stared at my chemistry assignment, but nothing was coming into focus. I wished we had a TV so I could plug in my brain and not have to think.

Finally I gave up. I was just dozing off when there was a knock on the door.

It was Sam.

He held out a plate. "Your mom sent me down with a piece of shortcake. Thought it might help you study."

"Thanks." I watched him set it on the table, glance around the cabin. "I wasn't really studying. Looking at chemistry puts me to sleep."

Sam smiled. "Chemistry, huh? There's one subject I always hated. I can't understand things unless they're right in front of me where I can see 'em."

"Yeah," I said.

He wandered around the cabin, tried the bathroom door, frowned at the crooked way it hung. "I'll have to come down here and fix that," he muttered as he came back to the table. "Say, did you remember to get me those stamps, Toby? Looks like I'll be up late, paying bills."

"Sure, I'll get them for you."

I went behind the curtain to get the stamps out of my jacket.

I was about to leave when I spotted my duffel bag lying in the corner. I paused, the book of stamps in my hand.

Sam was at the table, sampling the shortcake, when I came back out. "Here you go," I said, setting down the stamps. "And I think this is yours, too."

Sam picked up the magnifying glass. I saw him turn it over to check the glass, then run a hand over the mallard's head on the handle.

"I kind of wondered where it got to," he said finally. He pulled a piece of chamois out of his pocket and began to polish the lens. "I'm pretty fond of this old thing. I made it for my wife as a wedding present. She liked to read maps."

Mary Elizabeth Ryan

I watched his hand linger on the glass. After a moment, I realized he was looking at me. "You read maps, too, don't you, Toby?"

I nodded. "Yeah. I mean, I used to."

"Maybe someday I'll make you one of these." Wrapping the glass carefully in the chamois, he slipped it in his pocket. "But not this one. I'm glad to have it back." He stood up. "Kind of figured I would."

My face was blazing. "You did? Why?"

"Because you're a good kid." He paused. "I know it's been tough for you and your mom. But I want you to know I'm here for you, for both of you. Okay?"

I nodded. Sam pointed at the shortcake. "Try some," he said. "She's turning into a pretty good cook."

I wanted to say something—try to explain why Mom was being so nice, tell Sam he shouldn't get too attached, because sooner or later we'd be gone. But he was already heading for the door.

I reached over and tasted the shortcake. It wasn't bad.

From the door, I heard Sam chuckle. "That's a funny thing for a kid to take," he said. "A magnifying glass."

Sam cleared his throat. "That reminds me. Hal

Springer's been on my case about a little pair of Bushnell binoculars."

I froze. The shortcake dissolved in my mouth as I looked back at Sam.

He scratched his head. "He claims they got mixed up in our stuff on that fishing trip. I've looked all over, and I can't find them."

Sam smiled. "Would you do me a favor, Toby, and see if they're around? Maybe you'll have better luck."

"I'll take a look," I said.

"I'd sure appreciate that. Well, KP duty calls. Good luck with that chemistry."

After he left, I sat there picking at the shortcake, trying to fathom Sam Wilder. He wasn't like anyone I'd ever known. What you saw was what you got. When he said something, he meant it, good or bad.

I remembered the way he'd looked at me when we first arrived. Like he wasn't sure what to expect. He didn't look at me that way anymore. He trusted me. And he was asking me to trust him.

For some reason, that scared me even worse.

Saturday morning came. I waited until Sam and Mom had left for the farmers market. As soon as they were gone, I whistled for Edgar. I put him inside, locked up the house, and climbed on my bike.

By the time I got to town, the sun overhead had vanished and the wind had kicked up. I felt the first drops of rain as I parked my bike in front of the government building.

Sheriff Springer was at his desk, eating his lunch. No teriyaki today; sandwiches from home. I remembered the lunch that day at the river, and my stomach did a slow flip.

"Something I can help you with, Toby?" I watched him wipe his mouth and fish through his pockets for a toothpick.

I swallowed nervously. "Yes, I . . ."

The phone on his desk gave a loud bleat. I jumped.

Sheriff Springer paused, the toothpick jutting from the corner of his mouth. Finally he reached over and picked up the phone. "Yeah. Uh-huh. An accident? Slow down—let me grab a pen."

The sheriff turned away and began scribbling on a pad. He was definitely taking his sweet time, repeating everything as he wrote it down.

I licked my lips and waited. I leaned on the counter and stared at the door at the end of the room, where the jail cells were. If only he'd get off the phone—

I forced my eyes away from the door and

glanced around the room. Pinned on the board behind the sheriff's desk were a bunch of notices. They were right above the heating vent, and the forced air made the pages flutter.

"Jack? I can't make out a word you're saying." The sheriff sounded annoyed. "This blasted wind's screwing with the phone. Okay, one more time—"

Up and down the flyers floated. The sheriff was turning around, setting down his pen, looking my way. In another second he'd be hanging up the phone, walking over to the counter . . .

Everything stopped.

I stared at the top notice. The words leaped out at me: STILL AT LARGE.

If I squinted, I could make out the picture hanging above the sheriff's head, but it didn't matter. I knew whose face it was.

Get a load of this, her smile seemed to say. Catch me if you can.

I reached in my pocket. My fingers closed around the binoculars and drew them out. As quietly as I could, I set them on the counter and backed away.

I ran. Out of the office, down the hall, through the double doors. I threw myself onto the bike and rode off into the rain.

Mary Elizabeth Ryan

I had to get home. Do a Once-Over before Mom got back, before anything happened. . . .

The tires were slipping on the wet pavement when I reached the top of the hill that overlooked the town. My lungs were on fire. My head throbbed. I tried to remember all the people I'd talked to since we got here, all the stupid clues I'd left scattered like a trail of crumbs. Annie Chase was here. Anne Freeman. Still at large . . .

I pushed off, heading down the hill for home. When I reached the nursery, I dropped my bike and started running toward the cabin. Then I stopped. A familiar smell stung my nose. It hung suspended in the cold, wet air. I sniffed once, twice, and then I knew.

It was cigarette smoke.

Fred greeted me when I reached the door. I brushed past him and went into the cabin.

A garbage bag of stuff lay in the middle of the floor. Mom was in the tiny kitchen, pacing back and forth. There was a towel around her shoulders. Her curly brown hair was gone. What was left was cut short, dyed jet black.

She stopped pacing when she saw me. "We have to leave," she said.

"Where's Sam?"

Mom sighed. "We only got as far as Copper City. Sam decided to turn back, because of the storm. He's out in the truck now, delivering Easter orders to the farms near Donner. He won't be back for another hour at least."

The door slammed, and Fred came in. He went to the window and lifted the curtain. "You lucked out with this weather, Annie.

Bought yourself a little time. But not much."

I stared past Fred at the distant snowy mountains. A pain started low in my chest, under my heart.

"You don't have to do this," I said. "It's not too late. You can just—stop."

They both turned to stare at me.

"Are you nuts?" Fred frowned. "You think it's that simple? That she can just *stop*?"

I nodded slowly.

"Annie, tell him. Tell him what you've gone through to stay free so long. It's not something you throw away." His voice rose to an angry whine. "Don't you get it? She did it for you! Your mom wants to see you graduate. Have a life."

He wheeled to face Mom. "Well? Do you want your kid to see you led away under the TV lights, surrounded by federal marshals? Read your name in every paper? You want your son to go through that? Or your boyfriend?"

"Of course not—"

Fred shook his head. "You knew what the score was when you went under. No room for attachments, Annie. None. They're dangerous, they're stupid, and they'll get you caught every time. You can't screw up again."

"I know that," Mom said, nodding.

Fred reached for his smokes.

"Well, you'd better straighten out your son on a few points. I'm going out to the car and make some phone calls." I heard the scratch of a match as he crossed the porch.

"What happened?" I asked.

She was already finishing the Once-Over, taking things off shelves, putting them in the bag, feeling around under the bed.

"Fred says it's the little things that get you caught." She paused to pick up a hairpin and tuck it in her purse. "Could have been the license plates, maybe. All I know is that some old files were reactivated, questions have been asked. Fred got here as soon as he heard."

"Then what did he mean about screwing up?"

Mom stood at the mirror. I watched her rub the towel through her hair and then lean forward to study her reflection. For a moment her face softened. "I called my dad," she said. "I knew it was dumb. I just thought . . . well, I don't know what I thought. But it was good to hear his voice."

She picked up a lipstick and began to outline her mouth in dark red. When she was finished, the softness was gone.

Mom turned to me, all business.

"Come on, Junior," she said. "Let's get you

packed. Fred's made all the arrangements. We don't have much time."

I didn't move.

"Toby? You need to load up your stuff."

I looked at Mom. Guess who I am? she used to ask during all those trips. As if I ever had a clue. As if it even mattered. Her lips were pressed together impatiently, her eyes burning with road fever.

A wave of fatigue hit me like a fist. "No," I said.

"What?" Her voice was sharp.

"I'm not leaving, Mom." My voice wobbled. I tried to steady it. "I don't want to go."

Her mouth opened, and then abruptly closed. I saw the thoughts work around in her head. For a moment she looked torn.

Then, slowly, her back straightened as the survival instinct kicked in.

Mom reached for her makeup case and snapped the lid shut. "Fine," she said. "I'll send for you when I can."

The door to the cabin opened. It was Fred.

"All set?" he asked.

Mom nodded. "I'm ready," she said.

Fred finished tying up the loose ends on his cellular phone. A man named Charlie was coming by to take Mom to the next safe house. He didn't know where that was.

Fred hugged Mom. Then he walked up to me.

His eyes bored into mine, sharp and sad. "Do you know what you're doing? I'm not sure you understand what this means, Toby—"

"Don't worry, I know the rules. I won't say a word."

Fred shook his head. "That's not what I meant."

To my surprise, he hugged me, too. "Good luck," he said.

I stayed outside while they said good-bye. I watched Fred climb in his car. It pulled out of the parking lot and disappeared down the dark road.

When Mom came back, she was already different. It wasn't just the dye in her hair. Her eyes seemed to be a different color, her head held a different way. Jenny Parker was gone.

We waited in the greenhouse. Mom sat on the potting bench, the garbage bag of clothes at her feet. The place was dim, only the gro-lights over the houseplants casting an eerie glow.

Headlights arced across the glass. I saw my mother poise like a deer in the sudden light.

"I wish you were coming, Toby," she said.

"I wish you were staying."

Mary Elizabeth Ryan

"I'll get word to you. Or Fred will. This isn't the end of the world."

"I know," I said, even though that was just how it felt.

She was grabbing the bag, wrapping a scarf around her head.

"Mom . . ."

"I love you, Junior. We'll be in touch soon. Don't give Sam too much grief," she added as the car paused outside, its motor grumbling impatiently.

"I love you, too, Mom," I said.

But she was already gone.

After Mom left, I stayed in the greenhouse. The rain had finally stopped. I listened to the water drip off the eaves; the drops sounded like tiny footsteps. I tried not to picture her in that guy's car, speeding off into the darkness.

I thought of the Dumpster, all those rows of stupid plants she'd kept on the counter. They sat there for months, while Mom watered them and nurtured them and moved them around so they'd get enough light. And then one day, bam. See ya, suckers. Gotta go!

I stared at the plants sleeping under the gro-lights. They didn't seem concerned. They just sat there, dumb and trusting. They made me sick.

"Hey, she left you guys, too. Her little buddies. I bet you thought it would last forever. Well, guess again."

I started for the door. On the way out, my foot hit something. It was an African violet; Mom must have knocked it off the tray as she was leaving.

African violets are funny plants; you can grow a new one from practically one leaf. Mom used to pull over at a garden store and come out with these fuzzy leaves tucked in her pocket, grinning like she'd pulled off some major score.

Annie was here.

I picked up the square plastic pot and stared down at it. Then I opened the door and headed for the cabin.

I stuck the plant on the windowsill and then scoped out the room. She'd done a pretty good job, but I double-checked, just to be safe. I lifted the lid of the sea chest, felt around under the blankets. The box was gone.

I was about to close the lid when I spotted something. Taped inside the top of the chest was an envelope.

I peeled off the tape and opened it.

Inside I found a note and a picture of a man with a sunburned face. Big smile, squinting eyes. I couldn't tell what color they were. In the background were mountains. Pike's Peak, maybe.

I put it aside and unfolded the note.

*Junior—The box, the things in it, were supposed*

*to be yours. But now that you've seen it, I can't risk leaving it. Your paternal grandmother is Judith Chase Wright. She lives in Phoenix. She loved your dad and saw you when you were a baby. My dad is named Bob Freeman. He still lives in Philadelphia.*

She'd scribbled down their phone numbers.

*Please try to understand why I had to leave. I know you won't tell them anything. Toby, I'm sorry I wasn't everything a mom should be, that I made you live the life I chose, running from one place to another. I didn't know how else to keep you with me.*

*I love you XXX,*
*Mom*

I took the picture and slipped it into my back

pocket. I studied the phone numbers until I knew them by heart.

When I was done, I went to the stove and stirred up the coals. Crumpling the note, I fed it to the fire. I watched it burn until there was nothing left but ashes.


I was sitting at the table staring at a wildlife magazine when Sam appeared at the door. I didn't dare look up.

"Hal said to thank you for finding those binoculars," he said.

"Hal?" My eyes suddenly focused.

"I stopped by his office. He said you'd been there, but that you took off."

Sam paused. "While I was there, he showed me a fax. It was about a woman named Anne Freeman. A fugitive. It sounded a lot like your mom. If I know Hal, he'll check it out."

I looked down at the magazine. "She took off," I said in a flat voice. "She didn't say where."

Sam sat down at the table, too.

"Listen, Toby. My brother-in-law's an attorney in Seattle. I called him from town. If she turns herself in, he's willing to take her case."

Sam waited. I said nothing.

"I'll help you any way I can. Your mom, too.

But I won't hide her. If she's here, you've got to let me know."

"She's gone," I said. I shrugged. "That's all I can tell you."

Sam's face was creased with worry.

"I believe you, Toby. But you'll have to tell Hal that yourself."

We waited at the house until the sheriff arrived. I fed Edgar while they spoke on the porch in low voices. After a minute, Sheriff Springer walked in and sat down at the table. "How you doing, Toby?" he asked.

"I'm okay," I said. I set Edgar's water bowl down in the corner and patted his coat while he took a noisy drink.

The sheriff nodded. "Afraid there's some questions I need to ask," he said. He pulled out a chair. Reluctantly, I sat down.

"I don't suppose you know where they went? Your mom and her friend?"

I shook my head.

"The FBI's been called in. They'll be here in a few hours. News folks, too." Sheriff Springer took off his hat. He rubbed his eyes and sighed. "This is more excitement than this town has seen in a long time," he said. "Can't say I'm delighted about it."

"I don't know where she is."

"I'm sure you don't, son. But I've got a warrant to search the premises. Had to wake up a circuit judge to get it."

I pictured the sheriff rummaging through the cabin, through the sea chest, the duffel bag, under the beds and in the cupboards. It didn't matter. There was nothing left to find.

Sheriff Springer stood up. "I'm sorry about this, Toby." He paused. "Just doing my job. But I know this must be pretty rough on you."

I didn't say a word.

"Once we've located your mother, we'll see about contacting her next of kin. See that you're taken care of."

"Hal—" Sam stood in the kitchen door. "Why don't you take a look around, since that's what you came for. In the meantime, do you mind if Toby and I catch a bite to eat? It's been a long day."

"Sure thing." Sheriff Springer looked at me for another moment. Then he turned and lumbered down the steps, toward the cabin.

Sam touched my shoulder. "You all right, Toby?"

I nodded.

"Hungry?" he asked.

"What about the sheriff?"

"I told him you'd be staying with me for a while. In the meantime, I think we should see about some food." He reached for his jacket. "How does pizza sound?"

On the way to Copper City, Sam fiddled with the radio until he found an oldies station. I listened to Crosby, Stills, and Nash and watched the occasional headlights flicker past.

Sam squinted ahead at the wet road.

He shook his head. "This is wrong, what she's doing. She's got to come back and put things right."

"What if she doesn't?" I said.

"We'll worry about that when the time comes. Then you can decide what you want to do."

I wasn't hungry, but I ate most of the pizza myself. Sam watched me eat. After a while he got up and played some country music on the jukebox, wailing pedal steel guitar, lonely words. When he came back to the booth, he was frowning, the lines in his face sharp in the fluorescent light of the pizza parlor.

A loud bunch of kids came in and piled into the next booth. I listened to the twang of the music and wondered where Mom was.

"Weren't you ever suspicious about the things she said?" I asked. "The weird stories? How she was never the same person, one day to the next?"

Sam shrugged. "I just figured it came with the territory."

He picked up the last piece of pizza and smiled at me. "As a matter of fact," he said, "I kind of liked it."

"She made up that stuff about Texas," I said.

"I kind of guessed," Sam said.

"I never knew why we lived like that. I never knew any of it, until we got here."

"Kind of figured that, too," he said.


Edgar was waiting at the kitchen door when we got back. I opened it for him, and he raced outside into the rain. I watched him dash joyously around the yard, first one way, then the other, barking loudly, chasing ghosts.

"You can stay here in the house, if you like," Sam said as I watched him set up the coffee for the morning.

"That's okay," I said. "I've gotten pretty used to my mattress."

But that wasn't the real reason. I thought maybe she'd come back in the middle of the night, and I wanted to be there. But she didn't.

When I woke up, the cabin was cold, and I rolled myself up in a ball for warmth. Then I remembered Mom was gone, and why. I pulled the blanket over my head.

It was Easter Sunday. I've never had much use for Easter. Unless you're a churchgoer, it's just a time for painting eggs and buying chocolate bunny rabbits. But when Sam asked if I wanted to go to church with him, I didn't say no. It had to be better than hanging around the nursery. Waiting.

I hadn't been inside a church in years, not since the time we lived around the corner from a big Episcopal church, and Mom used to take me there to hear the singing.

Sam's was a lot smaller, but there were plenty of cars parked outside. He had lent me a sweater to wear over my good jeans, the ones that weren't ripping out at the knees. All the same, I felt weird when we got out of the truck and walked inside.

Sam led me to a seat near the back, but I still felt like the whole place was staring at me. I imagined they might be whispering: That's him, the fugitive kid. That woman, Jenny Parker—turns out she was running from the law. There always was something funny about her. I hear *Most Wanted Criminals* is going to come and do a show, right here in Donner!

Sam touched my arm. We stood up. I opened the hymnal and moved my lips in time to the words. There were more hymns, and then a sermon about hope and eternal life and resurrection. I didn't listen to any of it. All I could think of, the whole time, was Sheriff Springer digging through my duffel bag, studying my chess set for clues.

When we got back from church, an agent from the FBI was waiting with Sheriff Springer. He was pudgy and sweating, and he seemed to be in a bad mood. He asked me the same questions about Mom, I gave him the same answers. He took a look at the cabin, dusted it for prints, and left to file his report.

*Most Wanted Criminals* tried to set up cameras in front of the nursery. "We'll be running the story next week," the producer told Sam. "Should give your business plenty of recognition. Say, can we talk to the kid?" Sam slammed the door in his face. They parked their van on Indian Falls Road instead.

Easter dinner was roasted chicken with stuffing. Afterward, Sam tried to teach me to play two-handed pinochle, but I wasn't in the mood.

Instead, we sat in the kitchen and talked. About Sam's life before the accident. About mine before Donner; all the places, all the rules. It felt weird to finally tell someone, but Sam seemed pretty interested. Or maybe he just liked hearing about Mom.

While we were cleaning up the kitchen, I told him about the project for Hatcher, how it had led me to Anne Freeman.

"We're supposed to do a presentation," I said. "I've tried writing my report a dozen times, but it's still not done. And it's due tomorrow."

Sam looked at me. "Why write a report?"

"It's the assignment! Sunny Thieu did this essay on how her parents escaped from Vietnam, and I was supposed to come up with some research. . . ."

He handed me a plate to dry. "You have done the research, Toby," he said. "You've lived it."

"But—"

"Seems pretty simple to me," Sam said. "Just tell them the truth."

It got late. Sam cleared his throat and said that, considering what was going on, he'd feel better if I moved my stuff up to the house. There was plenty of room, he said. I went and got my duffel bag.

He showed me to the guest room and said good night. I got in bed and closed my eyes, but my brain was stuck in overdrive.

I kept thinking of the eager way Mom ran out to that car—ready to get away, to hit the road.

It made me wonder who she was. Was she the same person who took her kid to hear the singing at St. Mark's? Who, no matter where we lived, dragged me to see a dentist a couple times a year? Who made sure I had clean clothes, even if it meant lugging laundry on the bus, or talking some motel owner into letting us use his machine?

Or was she the mad bomber from Chicago?

A crack of light fell across the bed. Edgar padded across the rug and hauled himself up next to me. With a sigh, he flopped down, his thick tail thumping against my leg.

I sat up and stroked his big head. "This must have been Mark's room, huh?"

Thump. I made room for him, and he stretched out. I had a feeling he probably slept here every night.

"It's tough being loyal, isn't it?"

Edgar had no thoughts on the subject. He was just happy being where he was.

Pinned against the wall by a mountain of dog, I finally fell asleep.

\* \* \*

The bus came and took me to school. I kept waiting for photographers to pop out of the bushes, but the circus must have pulled out of town. No reporters, no G-men, no snoopy deputies. Just a gray Idaho morning, and a school bus full of sleepy kids.

Sunny was waiting at the door to Hatcher's room. "Are you ready?" she asked.

"Sure," I said. "No problem."

She squinted at me suspiciously. I brushed past her and headed into the room.

Kids stood around talking, but when I walked in, they fell silent. A couple of kids glanced at me, but I ignored them. I sat down and stared at my notebook until Hatcher clapped his hands for attention.

"Okay," he barked. "It's game day. I expect a good show." He gazed around the room. "We'll take these in chronological order. Who's up?"

One by one, kids trooped up and gave their reports. Every war the United States ever fought got sliced, diced, and dissected. One girl tried to slip in a report on women's suffrage, but the rest of the class played it safe. They knew Mr. Hatcher. Spanish American, World War I, World War II, Korea—every military action was present and accounted for.

Finally Sunny and I got up.

"Our project is on the Vietnam War," Sunny said. "For my report, I interviewed my parents.

They were born near Saigon. My mom's dad was a teacher, but they closed his school when the war broke out. My dad's family owned a restaurant. He got to know a lot of the American soldiers. When Saigon fell, he thought the Americans would take care of them. But my parents got left behind."

Sunny wasn't reading her essay anymore. She was looking at Mr. Hatcher.

"When the Communists came, my parents tried to escape on a boat, but it sank. Most of the people drowned. My parents were rescued and taken to a refugee camp. My sister was born there. She got sick, but there was no doctor, and she died."

There wasn't a sound in the room. Sunny paused, fidgeted with her glasses. Then she said, "It was really hard to interview my mom, because she doesn't like to talk about what happened. She says it doesn't help to remember those things."

Sunny folded her report. "I think my mom is wrong," she said. "It's like Mr. Hatcher said—history isn't just the past, it's part of us. So I think it's important to know what happened, where you came from. And even though it makes me sad, I'm glad I found out I had a sister."

Loud applause from the class. Sunny looked embarrassed. She ducked her head, and sat down.

Hatcher caught my eye. "Ready, Toby?"

I looked out at the blur of expectant faces. My heart began to slam against my ribs. Pretty soon they'd all know about Mom, what she had done, who she really was. Her picture would be plastered on their TV screens. Everywhere I went, there would be questions, whispers, stares. . . .

I saw Hatcher check his watch. I had a sudden urge to bolt from the room.

Then I remembered what Sam had said: Just tell them the truth.

"Sunny's right," I said slowly. "The Vietnam War still isn't over for a lot of people. As a matter of fact, it's the reason my mom and I came to Donner."

Hatcher was gazing at me intently. So was Sunny.

"Maybe you heard about those TV trucks parked outside Sam Wilder's place this weekend, and why they were there. If not, you can catch it on *Most Wanted Criminals* next Sunday. You can hear all about my mom. That she's this fugitive from justice. That she tried to blow up a recruiting center during the Vietnam War. That she's some crazy radical. Woman on the run. Wanted by the FBI. Armed and dangerous."

Whispers and murmurs raced around the room. Hatcher had his chin in his hand. His eyes didn't leave my face.

"But they won't mention the other stuff. That she's funny, and smart, and . . ." I stopped, searching for the word. "Brave. When she was only nineteen, she protested a war she thought was wrong, that her brother died fighting. She really cared about what was happening over there."

I couldn't tell if they believed a word of it. I took a deep breath and kept going. "My mom's big dream was to be an actress. She could have been a good one, too, but the only parts she got to play were after she went underground."

Here's the weird part about telling the truth: It makes you just as nervous as lying does. Just as scared.

But it makes you powerful, too. Different from the way I felt when I was stealing stuff. This was a whole new feeling.

Everyone was staring at me like I'd sprouted wings, or maybe antennae, but all of a sudden it didn't matter. I felt free.

"The other thing you won't hear is that she's a great mom. A lot of what she did, she did for me, so she could keep me with her, see me grow up."

Footsteps tapped down the hall. The door at

the back of the room swung open, and Mrs. Fields from the office glanced around the room. I raised my voice.

"Maybe my mom did the wrong things for the right reasons," I said. "Well, so have I; we all have. But she paid a big price for it and now she's trapped in this role she has to play. I don't know if it was worth it. But wherever she is, I'm proud of who she is. Proud to be her son. I only wish I'd told her."

No applause this time. Just shocked silence. I glanced back at Hatcher, but he wasn't looking at me. His head was turned, and he was staring at the open door.

Someone stood there—a short, slender woman with short black hair. I couldn't tell how long she'd been there, how much she'd heard. But I knew one thing.

It was Mom.

Hatcher recovered before I did. He limped to the front of the room and paused with his hand on my shoulder.

"Thank you, Mr. Parker. I think you've given us all something to think about." He picked up the chalk and began to write the week's reading assignment on the blackboard.

Some of the kids had spotted Mom, too. Heads

were turning, whispers began to ripple. I wanted to move, but I felt frozen to the spot.

Hatcher glanced up. He looked surprised to still see me there. "Toby? Why don't you head over to the library?"

"The library?"

He jerked his head at the door. "Beat it, Parker," he said.

I didn't stick around to thank him. I hurried to the back of the room, where Mom was waiting.

In the library, we sat down at a wooden table behind the reference section.

"They're looking for you, Mom. The sheriff was out at Sam's, and the FBI. Reporters, TV shows, you name it."

She wasn't listening. Just studying my face like she'd never seen it before.

"Did you hear me, Mom? You can't be here—"

"We got as far as the border," she interrupted. "I made him turn around."

"Mom—"

"I didn't understand at first. I was on that high of leaving. You know the one, Tobe. Everything gets very . . . intense." She shook her head. "When you told me I should just stop, it made me pretty angry. Because I knew I couldn't. I didn't want to."

"Then why did you?" I asked.

"They were taking me into Canada." Her eyes were rimmed with fatigue. She rubbed them hard, as if she were working to stay awake. "They said I should never see you again. That was the deal if I wanted to stay free."

She shrugged lightly. "Well, no deal."

I grabbed her hand. "Mom, would you just listen? We've got to call Sam. He said he'd help, and he means it."

"But Toby—"

I heard footsteps coming down the hall, heading for the library. I gripped Mom's arm.

"I don't care what those guys told you. Or what Fred says. You have to call Sam." I knew I was begging, but I didn't care. "You've got to turn yourself in, Mom!"

Just as the footsteps reached the door, Mom smiled at me.

"It's okay, Toby," she said. "I already have."

I am on a train. My eyes are closed, and the car swings back and forth. For a moment I let my mind go blank, so that all the thoughts, the feelings, slide off into nothingness.

Then the train hit a curve. I opened my eyes and looked outside.

Evergreens lined both sides of the tracks. A while later, they were replaced by the flat scrublands of eastern Washington. We were on our way to Seattle.

There were four of us—Sam, a federal marshal named Mona, me, and Mom. They'd wanted to fly us there, but Sam held out for the train. I was glad. It was big and comfortable and loud, nothing like the one in my dream.

The marshal was pretty nice, too. She kept calling Mom "ma'am," and offering to get us stuff from the café car. Mom wasn't allowed to leave her seat. Mona even had to go with her to the rest room.

Mary Elizabeth Ryan

At least she didn't have to wear handcuffs. Mona explained that was forbidden on interstate carriers. That was how Mona talked, like she was reading everything out of the federal marshal handbook.

I listened to the wheels spin along the rails. Sure enough, they made a clickety-clack sound. Just like in the movies.

After too many microwave hot dogs and cups of Amtrak coffee, we got to Seattle. Sam and I checked into a hotel near the federal courthouse. Mom didn't, though. When you're in custody, the government gives you a place to stay, free of charge.

That afternoon, Sam called his brother-in-law. He met with us in a little room at the detention center.

His name was Paul, and he looked exactly how I pictured a lawyer should look: tall, serious, wearing a great suit. I didn't follow much of what he said, since he talked like a lawyer, too. Just that he was doing a lot of research on Mom's case. In the meantime, he said, it was going to be a long wait.

Before Sam and I left, I mailed Sunny a postcard of the Space Needle. "You're right," I wrote her, "Seattle is pretty cool. But there's no place like home. P.S. Tell Hatcher I'm still working on our project."

The morning of our flight home, I sat in the little room with Mom. A corrections officer sat in the corner. I tried to pretend we were alone, but it was hard.

Mom pointed to the dark blue coveralls they'd given her to wear. "I told Sam he should get these things for the nursery," she said. "They'd be great to garden in."

"Mom—"

She smiled and touched my hand. "Try not to worry," she said. "And tell Sam to cut back the alyssum. It was starting to come into bloom. . . ."

"I thought people awaiting trial could get out on bail."

Mom shook her head. "Not fugitives, Junior. You can't really blame them, can you?"

I couldn't understand how she could look so calm. Happy, even. "But you wouldn't run anymore, Mom." Not a question.

She nodded. "No more running," she said. "We'll just have to see this thing out. Okay?"

The officer in the corner stood up and coughed discreetly.

"I wish you were coming, Mom," I told her.

"Me, too." She started for the door. Then she

stopped and looked back at me. "Oh, and Junior?"

"Yeah, Mom?"

"I'm proud of you, too."

When we got back to Donner, *Most Wanted Criminals* had run their segment on Mom. They closed by showing her picture with the word "Apprehended" running across her face. It made me pretty angry, but Sam told me not to waste my energy.

He was right. After a few weeks, people stopped driving by the nursery, slowing down to point and take pictures. I went to school, and helped Sam around the nursery, and waited.

The week school got out, he nailed up a hoop over the garage so I could practice over the summer. I figured it beat worrying, so I spent a lot of time out there.

I was out shooting hoops after supper one night when Sam called me up to the house.

"It's Paul," he said. "He's got some news."

When I got there, Sam handed me the phone.

"I can't promise anything, because it's all up to the judge," Paul said. He sounded excited. "But as far as I'm concerned, the government doesn't have a case."

For a moment I didn't say anything. I stood at

Sam's desk, gripping the phone. "What do you mean?" I asked finally.

"Ever hear of the Freedom of Information Act? A lot of stuff from the sixties and seventies was classified, buried in files that no one got to see. Until now."

Then he explained that back in 1970, certain agencies had infiltrated antiwar groups for political reasons. The person who hatched the ROTC plan and rounded up the explosives wasn't a student, Paul said. He worked for the government. The raid on the apartment wasn't an accident, either.

I felt dizzy. "What's going to happen to Mom?" I asked.

"Bottom line? She was set up, her name hidden in these files. Even that underground group never found it."

He began talking in legalese, about asking the judge to vacate the charges, fruit of the poisoned tree, tainted circumstance. I wasn't really listening. Underneath all those words, I knew what he was saying.

Mom was innocent.

They'd have to let her go.

It was over.

\* \* \*

Mary Elizabeth Ryan

On the ride to the airport, I was quiet. I was thinking about other trips, other lives.

Then I forced myself to stop. Those things were part of our old life. And when something's over, I don't drag it along for the ride. Sometimes the past is still like a garbage chute, as far as I'm concerned.

Let it go.

We parked near the terminal. I followed Sam up some escalators, down a long hallway. Finally we reached the gate.

I stood by the window as the plane lumbered to a halt, and they wheeled out the passenger walkway. After a long wait, people began to trickle off the plane.

A tall man with white hair emerged from the ramp. He didn't look very different from the other passengers: tired, a little dazed, carrying a small suitcase.

But I spotted him right away. Maybe it was the ears.

I felt Sam tap me on the shoulder. Mom was coming through the door. She was dragging a carry-on instead of her plastic luggage; her hair was different, dark red, curled in a short perm.

Some things never change.

She saw me and began waving excitedly,

beckoning me over to where she stood with the tall man.

"Dad," she said, "I'd like you to meet your grandson."

His blue eyes studied me. Even with age, they looked like they didn't miss a trick. I had a sudden urge to turn and run, away from this familiar stranger and his sharp blue eyes.

Then my grandfather smiled. "So this is Toby," he said. "So this is Annie's son."

I decided to risk it.

I smiled back.